I0593883

1.

Veta found herself a sixteen year old girl with her whole life planned out ahead of her, she had nine years of school, then the glamorous life of constant hours in surgery followed by retirement in comfort, at least that's the way she saw it. Those very thoughts had led her to this drunken realization that she was only sixteen, a young girl with naïve notions of the way an adult world was supposed to turn. No one had sat her down for the birds and bees conversation aside from her father describing a very uncomfortable sounding ritual between two people who Veta decided would never be her. She didn't know what it was like to be in love or to feel how other girls were always saying they did about boys. There wasn't any person that really tried to be in that kind of relationship with her, no matter how many hints she gave. In her current state the thought was enough to make her want to be sick.

Reed plopped down next to her on the bench seat at the window of his kitchen that looked out over a curved line of red rose bushes in full bloom. He had to search the house to find her in the first place and she didn't look like she was enjoying herself at all. "Are you feeling okay over here? You look seasick or something."

"I am a bit nauseated but I don't think I'll get sick yet." She smiled to reassure her lifelong friend, "Are you enjoying your party?"

"Truthfully?" he leaned into her ear saying in a breathy tone, "I would rather just hang out with you but Mom insisted." He pecked her cheek innocently, sitting back into the seat. His mother was well into her seventies and would never take no for an answer, it's why she had been allowed to spend so much time with him over the years. "Will you come in there with me? We can dance and I can introduce you to some of my friends and you might meet someone."

"Sure," she took his hand as he walked her back to the living room where everyone was dancing and laughing around them. A group of Reed's friends flagged him and he dropped her hand as quickly as he'd taken it without even looking back to see if she was following, maybe he didn't want her to meet those friends. He

3

searched her out to leave her alone again, this party got worse all the time. He hadn't spent any time with her thus far and because the kitchen was the hub of alcohol she was rather drunk and tired. She felt lightheaded and sat herself down on the couch crossing her hands in her lap and glancing around the room with little focus. In a big brown reading chair in the corner there was a couple making out obviously both intoxicated, to her left beyond the French doors of the hall was Reed laughing and carrying on with a group of guys that were dressed like the Princeton rowing team. There were people in every corner having fun, all save one. He was a dark figure leaning against the wall next to the kitchen, the black boots he wore were polished and shiny in contrast to his worn out black leather trench coat and dark jeans. In his left hand was a beer and in his right, a silver lighter that he opened and closed trying to entertain himself she guessed. Suddenly she felt like she had been looking too long and turned her head just in time for him to glance in her direction. When she got brave enough to look back he was gone. All for the better she thought since the mere sight of him had made her nervous on top of the rolling tide of being far more intoxicated then she had ever been before. She wished she could recognize even one face in the groups scattered around the house when someone sat on the couch next to her.

"Got any friends here or is someone playing a prank on you?" The dark man asked with a bit of a sly smile playing across his thin lips. He was tall with dark long hair that fell in his eyes when he turned his head.

"I'm with the host." She pointed Reed out to him on the dance floor.

"A kept woman?" he smirked lifting an eyebrow.

"No, not like that he's my friend and my neighbor." he had the softest brown eyes she had ever seen and they were smiling at her as if he knew her life story.

"Do you smoke?" She shook her head and he inexplicably took the same hand Reed had so easily dropped leading her out the back door to the porch, "Well I do and I could use some company." He said once it was lit.

"What's your name?"

"Max," he shook her hand and released it when she leaned towards the railing, "nice to meet you."

"Veta, pleasures all from mine." She stuttered a little.

"So you're Reed's friend huh?"

"I am." She was so nervous that she didn't want to speak for fear of stumbling over her words for a second time.

"He's a pretty cool guy I gather, are you in school with him?"

"I'm a senior at Madison academy."

"Really, me too, how have we never met?" He eyed her curiously blowing out a huge cloud of smoke.

"Pre-med studies don't leave me a whole lot of time for social activities and then I'm a teacher's aide as well." Her nerves were making it impossible for her to meet his eyes again and her legs felt unsteady on the wood planks that kept claiming the spike of her heel.

He flicked away some ashes turning to look at her, she seemed so young but she was in his grade, he couldn't remember ever seeing her before he would have remembered that red hair at the least, "Why aren't you talking to anyone?"

"I thought I was talking to you?" she wobbled a bit on her heels for a second time trying to pull them free.

"I meant before I kidnapped you." He stepped past her and sat on the porch swing hoping she would follow suit and sit down with him.

She shrugged, "Are you a real people person?"

"Can't say that I am, no."

"Then why do you ask if I am?"

He started to respond until her emerald green eyes looked down at him forcing him to clear his throat, "So you live around here you said?"

"Near Reed's parent's house in town, this is their cottage and ranch but I've never seen an animal any bigger than their beagle around here." She giggled at the irony.

"You actually know him? I thought you were making it up."

"Don't you?"

"I'm crashing this party," he cut his eyes to her, "you won't rat me out will you?"

"Being rather intoxicated and not all together sure I'll remember this, your secret's safe with me." He saw her sway a bit against the rail and took hold of her waist to sit her down on the swing next to him.

"I should tell Reed to put you up for the night, couldn't let you drive this way."

She giggled again, "Little chance of that seeing as I don't have a car yet." She laid her head down on his shoulder, he waited a few moments smelling vanilla and alcohol on her skin.

"Oh," His voice was enough to snap her back upright.

"I'm sorry, I'm just so tired."

"Can I give you a ride somewhere?" he wanted to make sure she was okay and no one took advantage of her though he couldn't figure out why he cared.

"I'll just go up to bed, it was nice meeting you." She got up from the swing carefully and walked back in leaving him alone on the porch. As she shut the door with one hand, Reed spotted her stumbling and excused himself from his group to come to her side.

"Are you having fun at all?" he asked both concerned and confused since he hadn't noticed that she was drunk before and thought for a moment that she may have been drugged.

"Too much, at least I drank too much." She giggled at the sound of her voice and he tucked an arm around her waist to carry her over to the same plush chair she had seen occupied before.

"I'm shutting this down, it's late anyway. Sit tight." He walked around the room clearing people out individually with a kind of care that only Reed could manage to portray, passing out his apologizes for cutting it so short and promising a raging party for the next visit. By the time he was finished she was long asleep and he lifted her gently to get her into the guestroom, after tucking her in he went around locking all the doors and windows when he heard a tap at the back door, "Who could that be?" he mumbled as he pulled it open, "Can I help you?" he answered with a smile on his face that faded as he took in the sight of Max.

"Yeah, I met a girl here tonight I wanted to make sure she got home safe but I never saw her come out."

"That's great, did you just want to tell me that or...?"

"No, she said she was your neighbor, Veta?"

Reed laughed involuntarily he tried to cough and cover it up, "I can assure you that after she's slept she will be fine." This scruffy guy must be kidding, how did he know Veta?

"Are you two close?" Max eyed him suspiciously.

"I could ask the same of you." He was obviously concerned for her, maybe they were friends. He relaxed his shoulders a bit trying not to intimidate him, "We're friends and she happens to be staying over for the weekend. Who might you be?"

"Max Glenn, I wasn't invited but someone told me about the party so I came."

"Doesn't matter, she's fine for now maybe check on her some other time." Reed closed the door and locked it resuming to close the rest of the house in the distance he heard a motorcycle start and leave.

That guy would be trouble for him one way or another and Max wasn't sure he was interested in starting a war with him. At least not over a girl he'd only just met, even if her eyes were the prettiest shade of green he had ever seen. Under the influence of alcohol she still had a very different aura about her than any other person he had known so far in his life and he was interested in getting to know her better if he could.

>>>>

When she woke up the next morning the house was brightly lit with sunshine and littered with cups, napkins, chips and ping pong balls. The tennis table was nearly half set with stale beer and someone had left their shirt on the porch. She pulled on a yellow pair of gloves and the garbage bags from the cabinet under the sink and started by gathering all the full ones and dumping them she was almost done when he came down the stairs rubbing his eyes and stretching as if he'd stepped out of the bed and onto the staircase.

 "We have a cleaning service you know?" he yawned watching her head shake as she went outside to clear the yard, "Has not had coffee yet, crazy person." He chuckled while measuring out grounds, her head was pounding but somehow she got it all clean before coming in to shower. Feeling fresher and less sick she saw him chopping fruit in the kitchen for a smoothie.

"Who is that for?"

"You my dear, the very first hang over remedy you'll try. Everyone needs a quick fix." He tossed strawberries and blueberries into the kiwi and banana he had already chopped into the blender. "Someone came to see you after you were asleep last night." He added ice and a splash of pineapple juice setting the machine to puree. Veta waited for it to stop thinking very hard about who she'd spoken to the night before.

"Can't imagine who, I don't remember talking to anyone." It was the truth and the last thing she could recall was staring at the confused girl in the window.

"Said his name was Max, he seemed worried about you for some reason but you don't even know him?"

"I don't, he's gone right?"

"Yeah," he dropped the subject, "How are you feeling?"

"Bit like I slammed my head in a door, my own fault I suppose. No one made me drink nine tequila shots."

13

"That is way too much, why'd you do that?"

"You ignored me most of the night and I didn't know anyone here and no one was overly friendly to me either."

"Or so you think, this Max was pretty interested in your well-being last night. He was also dressed like a teenage turtle sidekick." He shuttered at the memory of the dusty leather and greasy hair.

She huffed out a breath, "Did he really bother you that much because I don't remember talking to him and I have no idea who he is."

"I don't know it just didn't sit well with me."He handed her over a glass of his fruit concoction and poured one for himself.

"I'm sorry about that." He shrugged and rinsed out the blender with his back to her. "I really don't know him. I swear that's the truth."

"I know that's why it doesn't sit right with me." He turned back looking much calmer than a moment before, "I'm very protective of you."

"Everyone is, it's the 'why' that stumps me."

"You are a very sweet girl who could probably get me killed if anything happened to you, so it's personal."

She smiled, "That's a good answer, I've got to get home it's already three. Could you drive me now?"

"Sure, get your stuff." He watched as she skipped off looking close to her normal chipper self, Borris would be none the wiser to her wild night of drinking. At least he hoped that he wouldn't since that would quickly lead to him no longer being allowed to have her over. The trip was over an hour and they spent it singing along to the radio, making jokes and laughing. She would be busy the rest of the week, he was going back to campus on the weekend which meant they wouldn't see one another for a couple of months after that at the least. Neither wanted to talk about it at all and Veta had avoided the topic since the moment he'd arrived home for winter break, she didn't think he noticed but he had. "So I'm leaving on Saturday and to be honest I don't want to go, can you carve some time out on Friday for a meal?"

He never called it a date and maybe it never was, "I can manage a late lunch if we can eat it at the park between school and piano or we can watch a movie Friday night."

"Done." He kissed her cheek sweetly, "Try not to get into too much trouble between now and then."

She nodded an agreement, "You'll have to tell Dad goodbye then so don't forget, see you soon." She opened her door and paused for a moment, "we should set up a weekly phone call then too so we don't lose touch again."

"Sure, that sounds like a good idea." She got out and walked up to her house where a maid let her in and she went straight to Shea's room knocking on the door.

"Come in," she pushed it open to her oldest sister laying on her bed setting down a magazine, "What's up little sis?"

"I can't stand this waiting anymore, is Reed ever going to make a move on me?"

"He moved away to college, sounds like a big one away from you, forget him anyway he's so strange."

"He isn't strange, he's smart and caring, he never forgets my birthday or any other special occasion and he's such a gentleman even if I were lying naked in his room he'd return me to modesty with a stern talking to." She sighed looking to Shea for hope.

"If he means that much to you why don't you ask him out?"

"I can't do that because then he'll think I'm desperate." She dropped next to her sister on the pillow topped bed, "I'm not desperate yet."

"Do you actually like him?"

"Yes because he is my best friend, no because I don't think he likes me that way, I don't know how I feel really but Daddy seems to think he would make a good husband for me...someday that is." She watched her sisters pale face clear of emotion and began to fear what she may say next.

"He doesn't get to choose your husband Ylisaveta, you will pick your own if you want one at all. Reed is convenient and a very good friend to you but don't just date him because dad said to."

"I wasn't going to, he's just the only guy who treats me nice."

"Not a good enough reason either. Now get out of my room and go meet people."

"Yes ma'am." She really didn't know if she had any feelings for Reed and was starting to think more about this mystery Max then him at all. Why couldn't she put a face to the name, had she spoken to anyone? She did vaguely remember being outside but she couldn't place when or with whom made no difference anyway, she'd never see him again.

>>>>>>>>>>>.

Max sat against his headboard with a drumstick in his hand that seemed to hit the nightstand without any effort, that girl was still on his mind. That red hair on white skin had made him a bit weak in the knees though she was the one who couldn't manage to stay standing on the black heels that made her legs look like they never ended. How could she possibly be a senior in high school she couldn't have been older than fifteen and most kids that age were freshmen. If he had known that asking a bored looking girl to come outside would lead to him thinking about her for the next twenty hours he would have skipped the party all together. There was no way he was going to fall for this girl but he was going to check on her at school, just to ease his conscience.

2.

The next morning she got dressed in a white silk button up shirt and a black and white vertical striped fluted skirt, she spent a long time in the bathroom trying to get her hair to behave ending up having to just brush it out for the day or be late for school and there was no way she'd do the latter. Shea dropped her off and Veta stood at the gate for a few minutes before deciding to go in and get some tea. Most people were already eating their breakfasts around the long tables leaving the lines empty, she stood with her cup of hot water checking the tea bags to find anything that didn't say cinnamon on it.

"You did get home safe, I'm glad to see it," A nod was all he got out of her; "Booze must really loosen you up because right now I'm getting this very unwelcome vibe."

She picked Earl grey, "I literally know you by name and yes alcohol has been known to do worse things to personalities." She paid the lunch lady and took a carton of milk, turning back to him.

"Am I unwelcome?" he leaned in a bit trying to read her expression.

"Truthfully, I haven't decided what I think of you, my first impression is hazy to say the least."

"True to your word," her look said she wasn't following, "You said you wouldn't remember."

"Right I was. Did I at least act civilly?"

"We only spoke a few minutes, you were telling me how you knew the host."

"So...out of pure curiosity, why did you come back?"

"I felt like I should make sure you were safe I guess."

Safe was a word she was well acquainted with, "I was safe."

"I'm surprised you know about that at all, he wasn't exactly inviting either." He leaned in a bit closer to her again and she stepped back.

"Really?"

"If I didn't know any better I'd say he was jealous."

"Well you don't know any better, we've been friends all our lives."

"You keep saying friends he said friends, what am I missing here?"

He asked the right question and she had no answer for him, "You aren't missing anything."

"Can we sit or do you really like this cafeteria line?"

"I have a class to get to and honestly I don't have any idea what my relationship with Reed is, clearly it's complicated."

"I guess so, class is about twenty minutes away but I'm sure you're in a rush so enjoy your day." He flashed a smile and strode out satisfied in his inquisition that found her fine, if not a tad less sweet. She wasn't exactly what he thought at first but she did stand out despite the obvious way she tried to blend in.

The color of her hair was closer to burgundy than copper and those perfect almond shaped green eyes were brighter in the light of day, but it wasn't her looks that were different. The way she held her small frame and the personal care she took with her outfit, the first time that he met her she was in a tight slip of a dress that barely touched the top of her thigh slurring her speech and teetering on six inch heels now she was in another skirt much more suitable for school and dangerous shoes. Her face was stuck in his head making it clear that she would most definitely be an interest of his for a long time to come.

She'd had a long day in classes taking an extra course was starting to weigh on her a bit and yet she was still passing everything with a four and a half grade point average thanks to extra credit. She wasn't really a prodigy just a hardworking, fast moving girl who could retain large amounts of information more efficiently than most. After that morning she had a lesson and dinner plans with her family. She stood at her locker packing her bag when he walked up behind her again, "Need a ride?"

"Do you just go around giving out rides to every girl you meet?" she turned to him feeling rather irritated.

"Really depends on the girl and if I remember and I do," he winked, "you don't have a car."

"We spoke more than a second then I'd say." She flung her bag over her shoulder, "Sure, take me to my piano lesson?"

"Lead the way and I shall follow." She walked to the parking lot a step ahead of him the whole way as he hung back to check her out in motion before catching up to lead the way. When they got to his car he pointed and spoke first. "How long have you been playing piano?"

"Six months now and the next instrument on my list is the clarinet."

"Do you ever take a breath?"

"I've been breathing my entire life and we met at a party so I get out on occasion." Her cheeks were flaming red.

"Fair enough, so you do have other interests besides learning."

"I get tricked into hanging around the masses," she laughed and he couldn't resist a smile.

"Funny, you were a great table dancer so I guessed you were quite the party animal." He parked in front of the studio turning to her in anticipation of some kind of retaliation from this quick tongued girl.

"Well, I'm not, thanks for the ride I have one for the way home." She opened the door and stepped out.

"Guess I'll take the hint and leave you alone. It was nice meeting you Veta."

She sat back in her seat a little deflated by the impact her words had on him, "I'm sorry if I'm rude, Reed got all bent out of shape over you checking on me and I was still in a hangover haze. I will never drink again."

"Everyone says that after they've had too much. You...are a bit hard to talk to with all those walls up."

"So I should be giving you a chance?" she was intrigued by him to say the least. There wasn't a fake confidence that she saw so often given to guys by the car they drove or the money in their pockets, his was all real.

"That's up to you, in my opinion you should." He had a husky voice which made the words all the more enticing.

"Put it in reverse, let's go."

"Don't you have a lesson?" His head was tilted a bit confused.

"I pay for them, I can miss whenever I want to. You are getting a chance." She shut the door and set her sights on him.

"Right now?"

"I'm sorry are you too busy?" There was a challenge in her face that he didn't really recognize.

"No, I was heading to my garage to play my drums while the neighbors are at work. Unless you want to sit around watching me?" the cute little eyebrow wiggling he did had her laughing again.

"I think that sounds too loud for me. I have hypersensitive hearing and I don't like to be around a lot of loud music."

"That is downright crazy, how about I take you there to meet my brothers we're all in a band together and they skipped school today."

"They aren't in school with us?"

"They aren't in high school at all, Martin graduated but Matt and Mark are still in middle school."

"Well I'm up for anything, let's go."

>>>>>>>>>>>>>>>>

He dropped her off at home a few minutes before dinner was ready and she was left with so many questions about him. How did he get into music, why did he cook, why did all of their names start with 'M'? No use worrying about all of that now. She had a lot of

27

homework and a couple of more days before she was supposed to see Reed still she wanted to call him and talk about all of these new developments in the Max situation.

After they talked he wanted to come over and speak in person since he was concerned about this guy who popped up out of nowhere and now was trying to get closer to the girl he himself had chosen. Of course being chosen didn't mean she wasn't going to attract the attention that a pretty girl usually gets and the fact that she was unaware of being chosen wasn't playing to his favor either. In any event Reed felt he was being overstepped by this cocky guy who for some reason believed he was good enough for her. Had Reed had any time to spare he would have been there to talk it out but Friday was good enough since the week had only just started he would give the guy a chance to leave her alone on his own.

>>>>>>>>>>>>>>>>

"Veta, do you have feelings for me?"

"What do you mean Reed?"

"Do you ever think of me as more than a friend?" he tossed a couple of pieces of popcorn into his mouth. She couldn't tell if he was serious anytime he asked her a question and she didn't know how to answer such a straight forward question.

"You're my best friend, I don't know how I feel about you as anything more than that right now. Why do you ask?"

"These previews are boring and you have been sitting there smiling like an idiot at them for five minutes." He hit the pause button before the feature started.

"Can I tell you without you having a panic attack?"

"That depends, just say it."

"I like someone, I can't stop thinking about him." She sighed and looked at him for some kind of reaction but he was blank faced, his eyes were unfocussed. He didn't look mad or sad or anything else, "Say something please before I burst."

"Who is it?" he cleared his throat, "Anyone I know?"

"Well, you've met him. Do you want to know who it is?" she looked at him tentatively, "I know that you asked but do you truly?"

"I gather he doesn't have any idea how you feel, sure tell me." He straightened up waiting to hear one of the familiar names of the guys she hung out with at school or one of his friends from the party.

"Do you remember Max?" now she saw a reaction, "You don't like him."

"I don't know him though he's not what I would expect you to be into as far as looks are concerned. Can I ask a question?"

"Shoot."

"What got you so interested in this guy who just showed up at my party uninvited, might I add?"

"He stands out to me, against the background of our high society community he clashes in just the right way."

"Tell me you're kidding so I can breathe again."

"I'm not kidding at all, should I like someone else?"

"I don't expect to know all the inner workings of that twisted mind, how about you just tell me what it is about him that makes him so special?"

"He seems smart and driven, he is pretty nice but I don't know him very well yet. He's been around since elementary school and borders on Unabomber tendencies with his dark hair and cigarette smoke…" Her eyes were smiling and she just kept spouting things she liked about him, why not Reed? He was there every day if she had time for him, he had already put so much into her personally that he assumed she was going to start having feelings for him one day. Another girl like her wasn't going to be easy to find among these stuck up rich people. Reed knew it had to be a woman of wealth or no one, his mind was wandering and she was waiting for him to say something.

 "When will you tell him about all of this?" he asked without a thought.

"I don't know that I will, he's not exactly a friend yet, I don't know how he would react to a girl telling him she is interested. Nor do I want to be the kind of girl who comes on to a guy, I'd prefer being pursued." She was still happy to have those feelings even if she kept them to herself and she could see the relief on his face as he turned back to the screen tossing popcorn at himself again as if the conversation had only been in her mind. "Should we start the movie at least or stare at frozen blades of grass?" He hit the button and leaned back into the cushion to think while they re-watched an old favorite he bought for her and hid until he gave it to her on her birthday three weeks earlier. Hadn't he been pursuing her for the last five years this wasn't the first time he'd done something like that for her saving up his allowance a few times to treat her to an expensive dinner or backstage passes to a concert. To Reed she was the most beautiful and smart girl he'd ever known and she wasn't spoiled by her cushy lifestyle. He didn't know how to make himself any clearer they spent a lot of time with one another when they had it to spare but she was trying to finish high school in two years instead of four and he was in college a hundred miles away pursuing his own medical dreams.

She wasn't out of play until Max knew how she felt, so he could decide whether to turn her down or take her out. He was sure that nothing was going to make Max interested in Veta, not that he knew him well either but he didn't strike him as the kind of guy Borris would approve of. When the movie ended he glanced over to see Veta had fallen asleep with her head on the arm rest for a moment he stared at his closest friend with his thoughts playing cruel tricks on him, he set a blanket on her and backed out of the room. As he walked through her front gates he was thinking about how much time he may have left to ask her out, he walked into his own gates next door, when he got in he walked through finding his father standing in the kitchen with a hot cup of tea, "Did you and Veta have a good night?"

"It started well enough, Baba she likes someone else. Should I still pursue her or just leave it be?"

"When her mind is more mature she will see you are the better match. Don't fret anymore for now."

"Alright, goodnight."

"Goodnight son."

'Don't fret' was that the best he could do? She could belong to someone else any day now but he was hoping it wouldn't come to a fight since Max was easily thirty pounds heavier than him.

He got undressed and into his shower successfully washing his bad mood away, she wouldn't actually be with that ruffian by any chance. Her father wouldn't allow it. That was enough to get him to bed laughing at the idea.

3.

Veta spent some of her extra time planning a movie night full of all the new friends she was meeting in her pre-med classes, all of which were teenagers like her. The ones she invited she told to bring a date or their girlfriends, since most were guys. She straightened a poster on the wall, making sure that the pens she hung on each were still there with the instructions on voting for the feature film. She'd planned two movies and would pick the top vote getters from the five she'd printed posters for. A little game that made everyone feel included in the decision, a trick she learned from Dad.

The popcorn cart was popping its very first batch as couples started showing up. She loved hosting parties at the house, Dad had the theater decked out and filled with seats and comfy places the popcorn cart, which was something they used all the time, was in the hall with a stack of boxes for guests to fill themselves. On a table against the wall there was a long wash tub full of ice that she personally filled with as many different drinks as she could find at the store. As the last guest arrived and voted she was looking through the crowd all there in couples as she realized that she was the only person there without a date.

"When do we start watching movies?" a guy she'd met in chemistry asked with his girlfriend holding his hand.

"I'll tally the votes now if everyone is ready." She was met with most people saying they'd voted and everyone wanting to know the winners. "Of the five movies to choose from the first movie of the night is going to be... the romantic comedy, and our feature this evening will be...horror," they clapped filing into the room with refreshments to find a place to cuddle with their significant others. When the room got quieted down she dimmed the lights and started the movie wanting right then to call him. What was stopping her from inviting him to begin with? Dad was out of town and Trevor had been in his room with that blonde girl he'd introduced to her earlier...what was her name? Brandy? Barbie? Sandy? Oh what difference did it make, he wasn't going to leave her up there alone to check on Veta. She calmed herself and pulled the phone from her pocket, dialing his number from memory as always since she was afraid to leave it saved on the phone.

"Hey, what are you up to?" he answered in a hushed tone.

"I am having a movie night with some friends at the house and I thought you might want to come by and spend some time with me, if you're interested."

"Is Trevor there?"

"He isn't going to be around tonight. Come on, I only invited couples and I'll look like a loner if you don't show."

"I'll be there in five minutes." She hung up the phone to get him a drink from the table, taking it to the door with her to let him in before he knocked or rang the bell.

"This is for you, a nice lemon-lime soda." She giggled handing him the can.

"Thanks, my favorite. Are we planning on watching this movie?" Her only answer was to drag him along with her back into the dark room filled with couples kissing and almost no one watching the screen. The two of them had sat through a few awkward situations together but this was by far the hardest to bear. Despite their seven month long friendship the two of them had never kissed one another. They were embarrassed by everyone around them and he held her hand just to feel normal. He didn't notice it when she looked at their hands for a long time with her mind moving too fast for her to catch it. She'd never felt like they were on the same team before, true they were friends but it was always boys vs. girls to her even now that she was seventeen. It didn't help that he was her brother's friend as well as her boyfriend, a title she had given him in her mind since it was never established. Of course all the people around her were getting in and out of relationships all the time, in the end she simply hadn't thought of it for herself obviously not in the way they did. She and Max weren't dating in the way that everyone else seemed to be. In that short time of clasped hands she decided she wanted something more out of them something to make her see what all the other girls saw in the guys they'd chosen. Just as quickly as the thoughts came they were gone when he let go to put his arm around her shoulder, "Do we have to stay here with all this going on?" he gestured toward the room. She shrugged and let him walk her out and into the den. "That was strange, why would a single girl like you throw a couples party?"

"So everyone would have someone to talk to. I have no idea what I was thinking?"

"V, are you trying to say something to me with all this?"

"Let's get hypothetical here for a second. Let's say I wanted to be more serious with someone but I didn't know how to tell them? Hypothetically, what would you do?"

"I have never liked someone and not just told them." He rubbed his chin between his thumb and forefinger pondering. "I would tell the person how you felt before they heard it from someone else."

"I haven't told anyone but you that I even want anything to happen."

"You should tell him before another girl comes along talking faster than you can."

"Don't think that's possible." She laughed to herself thinking he hadn't figured it out at all. "Would you like a real drink? My dad has quite a bar in his study."

"No thanks," he took a step towards her and she took one away, "I would be interested in asking you to go out with me sometime."

"We go places all the time Max. What do you mean?"

"Would you like to go on a date with me, alone, not as a group?"

"Sure, that would be fun." She couldn't figure out how to react, should she ask how he figured her out or just be glad that he wanted to go on a date at all? He was an enigma wrapped in a riddle and she was laying all the cards out there like some kind of Hold'em dealer only keeping the river to herself till all the bets were in. "What brought this on, if I can ask?"

"I think I get what you said, and knowing you, you wouldn't have said those things to anyone but the person they were intended for, at least not in the way you said it." His hand went up to the side of his head as if he were trying to soothe a headache, no doubt brought on by the circular way she made him think. "The worst that could have happened was you turning me down. In that case we'd be talking again in about an hour so I wasn't set to lose anything."

"Really thought it through, I see."

"Some girls are spur of the moment types, some like to be surprised, you prefer to plan things out. I won't let you do that because I am coming to pick you up tomorrow night to take you out. " The smile on her face was all he needed to tell him it was going to be a night to remember. "Now let's get back in there before your guests start tearing the room apart." They went back to sit together in a couple of seats near the back of the room just as the feature film was beginning, it was scary enough to have her burying her head in her hands to hide. She missed the ending with a very scary moment that she actually hid from in his hard chest as he wrapped his arms around her to block out the sound too. The friends she had invited were ready to go home and filed out thanking her and telling her how great of a time they all had, she glanced over catching Max cleaning up after everyone.

"You don't have to help me, can I ask though, why were you so close when I called you live at least twenty minutes away?"

"I heard about the party and I was going to sneak in but you called while I was on the way so I didn't have to."

"Who told you about it?"

"I have my ways," he winked tossing a few cups into the bag he'd taken from the can in the back of the room. "No one spilled any drinks and I don't see any stray pieces of popcorn either. Are they all pre-med too?"

"At least half of them were."

"You are just a different breed of people."

"That we are."

He picked up the very last cup and set it in the nearly full bag, "I'm going to go ahead home but I'll pick you up tomorrow night at six."

"Okay, goodnight." Max walked out the door and she heard his motorcycle ride away from the house.

>>>>>>>>>>>>>>>>>>

"Did you just kiss me?" Her eyes were frightened but steadily gazed into his half scared and half amazed.

"Yes,"

"Can you do it again?" Before she could think he was there cupping her face as his lips touched hers and her eyes closed on their own as she parted hers deepening the kiss and igniting a fire in her that she had never felt before. His fingers tangled in her long hair to support

43

her neck that had gone limp. He tasted savory and sweet with a touch of tobacco but there was something more in it. He had done something to her that changed how she felt about him completely. He was still an arrogant, proud person but somehow he was just the opposite as well. Max could be humble under the right circumstances and sometimes for no reason at all, but she couldn't help but instantly connect with him. His tongue moved skillfully, whipping her head around into a nice cream and leaning back to watch her regain composure.

"I can do it again if you like, you know, in the name of science." His smirk was enough to make the butterflies do a fresh lap around her stomach.

"That'll do for now. I had a nice time tonight, we should do this again."

"It sounds like we have plans, goodnight Ylisaveta."

"Goodnight Maximus." He couldn't tear his eyes away from her slowly walking up the steps and into her house, seven months dating and somehow every date was a new adventure. He attended all of her performances and even the chess championship that she won, all the time she was looking better and better to him. She studied with a pencil between her teeth, grumbled when she didn't know an answer and slept with a stuffed bunny that she had once called Beadle. She didn't say any swear words and he couldn't bring himself to use any in front of her either. She was insanely cleanly taking it to an extreme he had never experienced before. It was also always a shock to see how sheltered she had remained in her childhood home protected from anyone who wanted to change that innocent perspective. As it was, he was only allowed in her house when her father was home to supervise in his overbearing way with Trevor, her younger brother, to enforce his rules. That man hated him without a reason since the moment they had met. Veta was a bit more excited than she should have been and somehow that labeled him a problem. Truth be told he wanted to be respectful to her for as long as they were together and he'd never push her into anything, half because she was too smart to manipulate and half because he actually respected her. She got along with his brothers and she was kind to everyone she met, he was impressed with her, who she made him want to be, but most of all he thought he loved her.

Nothing could scare him worse than that. In his mind there were three things that motivated him; the band, his job and getting to cooking school. Where was she going to fit into all of those plans? The next few days she would be in school and busy so he would be working as many hours as he could put in after school. Hopefully he could get a break from all the double work once these finals were over and he graduated, but first he had to get her to agree to prom. There wasn't any sure way to know that she would say yes but he hoped she would now that he'd scared off the competition with a few choice words. He thought about it with a rueful smile.

("I'm asking her and I don't care how you feel about it?"

"She doesn't want to go with you, look at how you dress. Can you even afford to rent a tux?" Max had to jam his hands in his pockets for fear of punching Reed square in the mouth.

"I can buy a tux if I need to, is that what you're worried about? I don't have enough money to be with her?"

"I just don't think she should be seeing a guy who rides a motorcycle and wears pony tails." Reed straightened his jacket buttoning the top.

"See, I don't want to get into this with you." Max stepped towards his car, "I'm asking her to go with me, we'll wear matching colors and I will buy her a corsage with a rose and everything. How does that sound?"

"Sounds like you'll have to take out a loan." He responded smugly and nearly set Max off.

"Watch it, how about you do the smart thing here and let her choose before you make an ass of yourself. I'll ask her and if she says no I'll let you know." Max opened the door getting in.

"I'm asking her first, she couldn't say no if you asked her then what chance do I have."

47

"Ask Cynthia and leave her alone." He pulled off and tried to put it behind him though somehow he knew that wasn't going to happen for Reed who would think on it for long hours trying to figure out how he'd lost the upper hand.)

4.

On the night of her senior prom she was the most excited she had ever been with a hint of nerves. Dali, the middle sister, had done her hair in a curly up-do that hung down her back, Shea was careful to put waterproof mascara on her long lashes. The turquoise taffeta dress she'd chosen was short enough to make her legs look infinite and long enough for her to dance as much as she wanted. Even the strappy sandals in their soft silver had a perfect shine to add to the night.

Her sisters never fussed over little Veta before and frankly she enjoyed it.

"Where are you going after the dance?" Dali asked in her sweet southern drawl she often saved for soothing people into her way.

"There's a party out at Reed's house that we may go to." Veta answered innocently.

"I think she meant after that too." Shea popped her gum and lined Veta's lips with a soft pink pencil.

"I can't say that we discussed that. I assume back here to drop me off."

Her two sisters glanced at each other with a look that always meant Veta was missing something that everyone else saw. "What?" she looked to Shea who turned away without a word. "Dalia, please tell me."

Dali cleared her throat, "Are you going all the way?"

"All the way where…That is ridiculous, you should both be ashamed of yourselves."

"She is!" Shea grinned suddenly pleased with herself.

"That's none of your business either way." She didn't find them quite so nice anymore, "Did you only offer to help me to ask that?"

"Maybe, on the bright side you look beautiful." Dalia spun the chair around so she could take a look in the mirror. A few curls touched the nape of her neck and she looked so natural yet enhanced, they made her hair sparkle with little crystals and Shea had done something she called a smoky eye that brought the green of her eyes to near piercing.

"We just wanted you to look nice. Hope you have fun." They both left the room as the doorbell rang downstairs followed by Trevor yelling for her to come down. She was stuck there gazing at a girl who so desperately wanted to be a woman without giving anything up to become it.

Slowly she descended the cherry wood staircase in a regal gait that had an easy smile on everyone's faces.

Max stepped to greet her at the bottom with a wrist corsage that matched their shared blue.

"How do I look?" she spun making her dress flourish a bit around her thighs.

"Wow." Max snapped a picture of her in motion, "that's one for the book." He slipped the ribbon wrapped flowers up her hand.

"Thank you, it's pretty." They couldn't meet each other eyes but he was looking at her while she looked at the floor, feeling very uncomfortable after her sister's assumptions.

"We should get going if we want to eat before we go to the dance." Max opened the door to see if she looked disappointed to see his car, she didn't at all, she looked delighted and he was instantly relieved.

"Couldn't get a limo?" Her father asked in a very disapproving tone that had Veta spinning around to give him the most severe look she could manage under the make-up.

"This is perfect, now we don't have to babysit a bunch of other people." She smiled again stepping into the door he held open for her. "I'll be home tomorrow morning." Borris huffed and threw his hands out before stomping off to his study as Max shut his own door and pulled off down her street, turning the corner before holding her hand.

"Where shall we eat?" He asked kissing her knuckles.

"Why don't we join the guys, where were they going?"

"Could we not hang out with those chuckling nerds? Who are they going with anyway?" He was on the verge of being upset about it when she looked at him confused about why he wouldn't want to hang out with their friends.

"I don't know, maybe no one or the out of town girlfriends they keep claiming to have." She shrugged, why had she mentioned them? "Why don't we pick up some fast food and park by the river to eat?"

"I like that idea much more." He made his way out of her subdivision, past the security building. "What should we have?"

"I just want fries, how about a burger place."

"You got it." Their hands sat entwined in her lap the whole drive and she stared at how much smaller hers were, she was always staring at his hands. He had short clean nails and his grip was gentle but commanding. She felt like he wanted to claim her, as Shea had so boldly suggested just a few minutes before. She couldn't conjure a memory of him being anything more than friendly. They'd only been on a couple of real dates, otherwise there was always another couple or a group of friends to keep things light and fun. At school the usual cast of characters was always present in and out of classrooms. The only other time they had ever been alone was when he'd driven her to his house to meet his brothers. She had barely spoken, he made her so nervous. The car made its way up the drive-thru of a popular place with seasoned curly fries and he ordered two along with a big drink to share.

Veta sat with a smile playing on and off as she was so far away in her mind, he squeezed her hand to get her attention, "You feeling okay?"

"Yes, you have big hands...I'd never noticed before."

"Is that supposed to be a compliment?" his eyebrows knitting as he pretended to think it over, "I'll take it!"

"Typical me, always off in the distance thinking about things that don't matter." She flushed feeling foolish.

"My hands matter to me," he tightened his grip a bit on hers, "Thank you." He let go to grab the cup and bag from the window. "So now to the river..."

She couldn't help but hear the hidden enthusiasm behind the words, "To the river." She pointed trying to play navigator. "Can I have the bag? It's bound to get cold if we aren't hasty. Cold French fries is the worst taste in the world." He handed over the bag with a laugh and watched her as she pulled his out first to put in the cup holder.

"Are you coming to graduation next weekend?"

"Of course, I'm graduating too." He had completely forgotten.

"Would you like to go somewhere after the ceremony and talk about us?"

"What do you mean by us?"

"Well, I have to keep working for a while before I can afford to go to that culinary school I got into and I have to find a place to live too. I thought maybe we should move in together." She didn't say a word just stared at him with a French fry in her mouth. "We don't have to talk about it now but I do want to have the conversation at some point."

"Okay." She smiled thinking to herself about how suddenly everything always happened with Max. Once he had something on his mind there wasn't a way for him to divert from the plan at hand until it came to the end he wanted. It's why she believed in his band making it at some point since he wasn't all together focused on that project or else they would already be someone. They got back into the car on their way to the dance that was in a reception hall of hotel near the school and they had to show student id to get in. The pictures were taken at the top of a faux ivory staircase and they went up first so Veta could take her shoes off afterwards. Together they spent a long time on the dance floor laughing and enjoying their friends' dates. They had each shown up with someone and they were all the most delightful girls you've ever met. They also knew one another somehow. Max called them 'the three hookateers'. Reed was there with his new girlfriend but he managed to keep his distance and stay out of Max's line of vision. The night was going so well that she forgot about all the things Dalia and Shea insinuated and actually ended up having a lot of fun.

"Are you tired yet?" he said into her ear seductively.

"Sure," they made their way off of the dance floor and he got a couple of glasses of punch. "I thought we were leaving."

"Not yet, let's just take a little breather here then get back out there and dance some more. We have time tonight." He smiled handing her the plastic teacup filled with pink punch.

"I suppose we do, no one is expecting us anywhere until Reed leaves at least."

"Don't remind me, are we still going to that?"

"You know what, enough secrets, you won't tell me what happened, he won't tell me what happened and I need to know because you both mean a lot to me."

"This won't affect your friendship with him, just mine."

"But I'm with you. He's my best friend and I don't want to lose either of you or have to hang out with you separately. Just tell me and I can fix it."

"You are it. Reed told me that he wanted to be with you as well as some other things I didn't want to hear." His free hand balled into a fist again at the memory of wanting to knock him out.

Veta was amused and thought he was telling some tall tale to stop her line of questioning, "Oh and when did this happen?"

"A week before I asked you to the dance he asked me if I thought it would be a good idea for him to ask you."

"May I ask what you said to him?" she was beginning to think he might be telling the truth.

"I said he had a better chance with Cynthia Bloom then you and that I was planning on asking you. He got rather offended at that point and said he didn't want to go up against me but he wouldn't hang out with me anymore or something to that affect."

"How long has he been seeing Cynthia?"

"Since two months ago about when this happened, why do you ask?"

"He's been talking about her with me for a couple of months. She may have been his intended all along." Max kissed her cheek and pointed as Reed left the dance shaking hands and reminding guests about the party.

"He's so in love with you V, he made sure he made it your prom. I know you aren't going to just leave me right now but one day you'll see that he will always be around and better than me."

"Don't talk that way, Reed is like another brother to me. He knows me better than I do and he has been so nice to me over the years when I'm little more than an annoying little sister."

"You are so blind to reality sometimes, especially for a person who is supposed to be grounded in it." He took her hand standing to go back to the dance floor and change the subject. They announced winners for prom court and Max pinned a little tiara on Veta's dress when she was given a princess title. He'd planned on giving it to her if she won queen but she was so happy for the winner that he couldn't help but crown her anyway. She was a very unique person with a soul that showed right through her at times. He wanted to photograph it one day, the glow that shown out of her, visible to everyone but her. A slow song had him holding her close and swaying back and forth along with the crowd. "Can we go to the party now?"

"Right after this song," the comfort she felt up against him was something she'd never experienced before in all her life, he radiated a heat that had her cuddling in for more as the song ended. "If you don't want to go to the party we can skip it." She was being coy and baiting him somehow but he didn't care. He waited for the song to end and led her towards the door.

"Where should we go?" they walked outside into the humid May night.

"The car first I guess." She knew where it was parked and went to her door he was a step behind and touched her cheek gently to turn her face to him, memorizing each little speckle of color as she reddened under his observation. He leaned in just touching his lips to hers in a sensual kiss, she parted her own welcomingly. Everything to her was exaggerated his fingertips tracing her jaw line rose goose bumps over her whole body, his other hand firmly in her back so she couldn't move away. She felt warmth in her cheeks and her heart with his body pressed against hers, she could see fireworks bursting behind her lids, a song played in her mind and the taste of him lingered on her tongue.

Max growled, "How did I wait so long for that?" asking himself aloud before claiming her mouth again in another long, lingering kiss.

"We...should go somewhere." She whispered once he pulled away to kiss her neck.

"Where should we go? My brothers are at my house waiting up to question my judgment. Your place is packed full of siblings." He looked at her with a bit of helplessness.

"We could get a hotel room, you could get a hotel room I mean. I'm not old enough."

He didn't answer, thinking it over "Sure, let's go." He started the car taking her hand over the armrest. The first place he came upon was old and broken down, he passed it finding a cute little inn on the side of the road. He went in chatting to the lady behind the counter as she charged him for a night in a single bed room under Martin's credit card. He began banishing all of his expectations, she was going to have to call the shots. "Got the key to room fifteen, she said it was around this building. Are you sure this is where you want to be?" He sat down in the car trying his best not to talk her out of it while still being honest when he thought she could be nervous.

"Yes, we're here. We got a room." She had a smile on her face but since he didn't understand her completely he went with it.

"Around the corner we go." He was nervous too but he wasn't going to tell her that. "Here we are," as he parked, she was already standing outside of her door.

"Come on." She took the key and went into the room ahead of him to wash her face and hands in the sink. The room was clean and the bed looked freshly changed. He glanced around as he stalked her. She didn't hear him come in to the room or look into the mirror to see him as he snuck up behind her.

"You look prefect, stop trying so hard," as he wrapped his arms around her waist to put his head on her shoulder. "Let's just go sit down and watch some TV."

"Sounds like a good idea to me." It was a springy king sized bed covered in a dark bed spread. His hand was still on her hip as he pulled her closer. His smile was sweet and cunning he wanted to be the hunter tonight in a way that made her ask him to take her. She was comfortable with him, laying her head on his shoulder and her arms around his waist. Her hair tickled his arm and he brushed it away to kiss her neck ever so slightly listening to the soft sigh it caused to catch in her throat. She smelled like sugar and tasted just as sweet. She was the most supple, warm woman he'd held. Her kiss was yielding and insistent it answered his in rhythm and need. He unbuttoned the dress she wore from the bottom, one little button at a time his hands slipping under to touch the warm flesh of her back.

"V, you're amazing."

"What?" She whispered out of breath.

"I have no idea, I've never been this way with you I never wanted it before tonight." He tipped her head back to expose her throat, "Tonight, you smell like candy and look beautiful, I just don't want to cause some kind of problem between us unless it's worth it." He nibbled at her raising the goose bumps afresh. She couldn't find a word to use and decided to kiss him instead, shrugging off the unbuttoned dress to her hips, to reveal a gold colored brazier made of lace. She put her shaky hands up to his chest, he was so firm with his sparse hair and lean muscles she never would have guessed were under the layers of tattered black shirts he wore. He couldn't keep his hands off of her taking the bra away letting her ample bosom spill out freely. "You have the softest skin I've ever felt."

"If you keep complimenting me I'll never be able to stop you."

"Even better," he pulled her down with him onto the bed, hovering over her. "Not that you want me to stop do you?"

"Mm not yet no," she flicked her tongue at his bottom lip as his hands roamed her body. He was left with the control he wanted but she still hadn't said the words and he'd go no farther until she did. His mind had been made up the moment he handed over his brother's credit card at the front desk. This was far from a flippant decision and he wouldn't make it alone not even to get what he wanted. Still she was lying there in his arms surrendering herself to him, her skirt gathered around her slender hips with a hint of the matching panties showing beneath it. He balanced on one arm taking in the scene before him. She was innocent and still so perfect and untouchable, her ivory white skin like silk under his fingertips. Her curvy body fitting with his in a comfort neither had experienced before.

"What should I do? There you are, here I am what next?"

"Be gentle with me Max." she purred trying her best to be alluring.

"Don't talk like that or I'll have no self-control at all." He nipped at her neck, kissing along her jaw and back to her tasty mouth. He made her swoon with each touch of his hand sending her into a shuttering frenzy. He kissed, moving with her as he took her over the edge. Suddenly she was glowing she recognized the stunned look on his face and took over easing him onto his back, to climb up and straddle him. She nibbled his ear lobe, kissing him a few long moments. "V, I want you, right now."

"Take me." She whispered in his ear. He took her at her word and pushed her back to the mattress tearing her underwear from her and pulling his own pants off as quickly, his deep inhale had her on edge as he positioned himself over her.

"I'll try not to be rough with you but I can't make any promises." She nodded as he covered her mouth in a savage kiss, would she never get used to that dizzying feeling that came over her? He slid into her in slow motion, fireworks again before her eyes and nothing was complicated about it. His hands in her hair with his arms behind her, held her up to him as he tried to steady himself with his teeth dug into her flesh, he felt the way her heart was racing, the tightening of her muscles as she adjusted to the pain and he enjoyed the smell of her sweat beaded skin. He even, for a moment believed that he had heard her thoughts in his own mind. Seconds were minutes, minutes were hours and he spent them all indulging in her, feeling all the subtle textures of her, the way she moved beneath him. He wanted to touch every inch of her and make his mark, one worth remembering and big enough to be seen.

He couldn't let her go, all night he held her close to him still naked and wrapped in sheets, as he lie there smelling her perfume mixed with his after shave, something happened and he knew there was going to be a very different relationship between them. He'd been with two other girls in his life but neither of them was anything like her. The only option he was left with was being with her, it sounded too good to be true.

Her father allowed them to date. He had let this happen because she said she liked him and no one else was good enough as far as she was concerned. Still he didn't understand why it had taken her so long to say it if this would be the end it came to. He couldn't remember whether or not she had ever talked about any other guy she liked or wanted to date, at least not to him. The only competition he ever had was Reed and honestly that was a long way from a real battle as he stepped down only seconds after being told that Max wouldn't. Somehow she was still friends with both of them without any issue which made him wonder if she may have already known how Reed felt. She had even managed to get the two of them together in the same room for a couple of occasions that she wouldn't celebrate without both by her side.

She rolled her back to him tugging his hand between her breasts where she held it clasped in her own. He belonged there, at the very least for that night he was right where he was supposed to be, holding his best friend, his confidant and most recently his lover close to him.

5.

She pulled up in the driveway of their two bedroom love nest with a stack of books and a bucket of fried chicken, Max opened the front door for her as she got to it. "Hey babe, how was school?"

"Exhausting, but that could have been a side effect of all the hours I stayed up last night, nothing I can't handle." She dropped her purse and set the books on a table to dig into the bucket. "I have ten hours to learn the entire circulatory system's Latin names and all I want to do is eat chicken." He grabbed himself a drumstick.

"Got to learn this stuff sometime right?"

"Yes, I just want to grumble then I'll study." He planted a kiss on her forehead and walked back to lounge on the couch and play a football game. Veta hated the music so he had it muted as soon as he saw her headlights hit the window.

"Do you have any free time tomorrow night for Janet's party?"

"I forgot all about that." Her hand went to her forehead, "If it's after five I can go for an hour or so...Is it the engagement or bachelorette?"

"I assume engagement since we are both invited," frantically hitting buttons to make the touchdown, "Yeah."

"Okay we should make time then. She is my classmate anyway...I have so much to do, this sucks."

"Of course it does, this is the part you look back on in ten years when you're a famous brain surgeon and think 'thank God it only took nine years."

She collapsed into his lap making him hit pause in the middle of the kickoff. "Yeah, well I could really use a shoulder rub if it's not too much to ask." Her adorable lips pouted out and she cut her eyes sweetly clutching her hands to her chest.

"Fine, sit up," he shoved her playfully out of his lap resting his hands on her shoulders to rub gently. The friction started to heat up her vanilla scented lotion that always drove him wild, he kissed her neck brushing her hair aside to bite gently.

"I like where this is going but we'd have to be really quick so I can get to studying and that's no fun."

"Ah, I agree. Go study before I take you." He turned her head to kiss her lips then shoved her away. "Go finish so I can have my girlfriend."

Veta studied for hours, copying over anything she thought might slip free. When she was finally ready to call it a night she found him slumped over on the sofa cradling the controller in his lap. "Maxy, get up and come to bed with me."

"Alright," He rolled off setting the remote on the table and dragging his feet all the way up the stairs, plopping flat on the bed, "Night V."

"Goodnight." She crawled in and fell asleep before her head hit the pillow.

Every morning with Max was an adventure. Veta woke up to the smell of eggs every Friday, he would wait to brew the coffee just so she could smell them frying in the pan. Once she showered and got dressed he would make her scrambled eggs and bacon. The whole house would smell for days but it was so perfect. She knew it was Friday and what was on her schedule as soon as she sat down because he always put out her planner to the correct date trying to save her time and sanity during a grueling school year. They ate breakfast together every day, even if that meant that one of them had to get up early to compensate for schedules, even if Max had to come in by video chat from the studio. It was a nice arrangement where they both felt comfortable compromising for one another. "I've got a really long day ahead of me, studio recording and a live show tonight, I am going to be dog tired." He shoveled in a forkful of eggs.

"Nah, you'll be so pumped on adrenaline that you won't sleep for weeks." She giggled seeing him nod in agreement enthusiastically. "Wait didn't we have Janet's party tonight too?"

"Yeah, it's before the show so I'll be popping in for an hour or so then heading on."

"Can I pretend I'm going with you?"

"Just come. It's just music, it's not going to hurt you."

"Nope, just my perfect hearing, no thanks mister, have fun." She served up her own breakfast and filled her favorite mug. "I've been to a few of your shows. Your music is great, it's just so loud." She sat on the edge of the window seat to eat as quickly as possible and get to school on time.

"We have some mellow stuff too."

"Yes, but the other problem is you play in crowded nasty bar rooms." She shook her head hoping to get the image out of her mind and convey her point.

"Clean freak," he rinsed his plate setting it into the sink, "I have to go, good luck on your test. The party is at six so please be ready." He kissed her roughly on the lips and hustled out the door, followed shortly by her heading to school.

>>>>>>>>>>>>>>>>>>>

Veta was studying at the table after she left the party that Max hadn't managed to show up to, she couldn't focus and her head was starting to hurt when she heard his bike pull into the garage, "Hey, how was the show?"

"We got signed!" She was shocked and stared at him for a few seconds letting the words sink in.

"That's great, when do you guys start? When does everything start I mean?"

"In the next few weeks we'll be doing studio recording, real studio V!!" He could scarcely contain his excitement.

"I'm so happy for you guys. I sure hope you're a sensation." The smile on her face was bright enough, she'd even taken care to let it wash over her and possibly forget the fear that bubbled up inside of her.

"We'll have live shows and groupies, we are going to be opening for big names for the first year or so to gain some momentum. Can you imagine all the people that will see us and want to be us or do us? We are on our way. Dis-Integrated; in giant letters on LED screens around the world, London, Amsterdam, and China, with all those people screaming."

Had he forgotten who he was talking to in the midst of his joyous ramblings, "Everything sounds rather up in the air, wouldn't you agree?"

"Well no one is taking chisel to stone yet, if that's what you mean. Would be more so once we had our own tour, we could plan our venues and things like that." He finally saw the sullen look on her face that she gave up on hiding once he'd mentioned groupies and been pretty obvious about his intent. "Aren't you the least bit happy for us?"

"Please Max, of course I am, just realizing how long you're going to be gone, how many fans I'll have to compete with, that's all."

"I don't see how there would be any competition since we couldn't possibly stay together when we're both so busy." He had thought that he'd feel relieved once he said it out loud, instead he saw the worst thing he'd ever laid eyes on. The strongest girl he had ever met with her hands limp at her sides, her mouth was held closed by clenched teeth and her eyes were dead. She could have been thinking any number of murderous things but wasn't thinking at all. She had no idea what to do and how she was going to get back home. She was lost and scared and so many other emotions but nothing was showing behind her perfectly still eyes. What had he done?

>>>>>>>>>>>>>>>>>>>>

The front door swung open to her empty house. Her bag was pretty heavy but nothing compared to the weight of her eyelids that slid down time after time. Figuring she couldn't fight them much longer she trudged up to her bed and dropped lazily onto the down comforter. Why had she decided to drive home from school? It'd been such a long day and the drive took all the rest of the energy she had.

She was just eager to see her own things even if there wasn't anyone to share those things with. Veta was adjusting well enough to single life without any real sadness or thoughts about it. He never crossed her mind when she was working and had no place in her unconscious mind either. She scarcely realized the distraction was gone since diving so deep into her work. Seemed that she would be alright, no matter how things turned out. No doubt he was doing the same...

Matt was strumming along on his acoustic to a song only he knew. Martin was lying with his arm over his eyes to block the sun streaming through the RV's windows, Mark was driving, extremely annoyed with Matt's constant noise. Max was tucked into his bunk with his phone, trying to text her discreetly.

"What's up?" He clicked send and spent another second to silence his phone. It lit up.

"I'm trying my best to stay awake, how about you?"

"Heading to L.A. Everyone is trying to sleep."

"Shouldn't you?" He tried to think of the exact reason he couldn't.

"Can't stop thinking about you long enough to sleep."

"It seems to me that I am more of a nuisance than anything else." Why was she being cynical to him when she felt the rush of heat to her cheeks?

"Ha-ha, yeah maybe you are."

"I could leave you alone, but you messaged me first."

"Can't leave me alone now, how's home?"

"COLD."

"That is not what I meant."

"I'm still working, it's okay."

Matt snatched the phone from his open hand, "Are you really talking to some girl right now?" Matt opened the message reading Veta's name, "This had better be a typo."

Max stood from the bunk snatching his phone back, "It is none of your business who I talk to."

"That girl is fucking poison man. You are crawling back for another taste though aren't you?"

"Shut the hell up!" Mark yelled from the front of the bus, "Who are you talking about anyway?"

"He is talking to that Russian girl again." Matt said and Martin popped up, hitting his head on the ceiling.

"What's wrong with that?" Max had no idea what they saw about her that he didn't but it must have been awful for this kind of reaction.

"Again?" Martin rubbed the bump rising on his head, "You get all happy and bouncy, doing all the happy Max stuff then just as fast you're sad Max there isn't really a decided middle ground, she's a puppeteer of your emotions."

"Good analogy." Matt slapped his knee, "So we are all agreed? No Veta."

Martin raised his hand. "I'm pro-Veta myself, she's hot."

"None of you get to tell me who I can and can't talk to, or date. Thanks though Martin I'm pro-Veta too."

"Split vote, forget about a tie breaker."

"Don't fall in love with her again man. She's just not right for you." Matt walked to the front to sit in the passenger seat next to Mark.

"What is their problem?"

Martin slid down to sit across from him. "I have no idea because when you guys broke up you wrote an entire record in a day."

"She's not the one who broke it off, it was me."

"Don't think that matters. You were still way down for a while afterwards."

"Is the music still good?"

"So that's why Marty picked pro." Mark chimed in.

"Sorry to dash everyone's hopes but we are just friends."

"Sure." Said Matt

"This conversation is officially over." He looked back to the screen to see another message came in during the nonsense.

"When will you be coming through?"

"Couple of weeks from now, why?"

"Could you get me a few tickets for some friends?"

She didn't include herself and he thought about how she never was fond of his music no matter how many times he tried to get her to listen, "Sure, just three?"

"Four, if it's not going to be a big problem for you to get them."

"No problem at all, pick them up at will call before the show."

"Thanks."

"She asked for tickets to the show for friends. You guys satisfied that we aren't dating?"

"Friends, sure, she's coming to the show." Matt complained under his breath.

"You really think so?" He asked hopefully.

"Do you want to test her? Don't talk to her until we know if she is coming to the concert. Don't message first and only respond cordially." Martin suggested.

"We have ten shows planned between now and then. I don't even really have time to think about her."

"That's how you explain it later. Just ignore her now." Matt agreed and Mark nodded along, tipping the scales in their favor.

"I'll put the phone down as soon as I secure the tickets."

He kept his word and Veta was left waiting to hear from him, if she showed up at the theater. Someone said the tickets had been picked up but he still wasn't sure how he would know if she had done that herself or someone using her name. He should have included backstage passes, why hadn't he thought of that? Max found himself standing at the curtain watching fans find places to stand. He had no idea where she would be, this place was standing room only. He tried to figure it out logically, she wouldn't be near the front where so many people moshed and smashed into each other, she wouldn't be wearing anything that resembled the rest of the crowd and there was no way she would stay with her friends who were supposed to be fans. He also kept wondering whether she'd intended to come at all. The message was so vague every one of the countless times he'd read it, never seemed to be very clear. Dropping the curtain he set up his high hat behind his drum set and sat a few inches closer to the stage's edge. They were the headliner tonight and some girl couldn't change that just with her presence or lack thereof. Martin was already saving his voice for the night ahead and had a handy notepad and pen that Mark always wanted to make him eat. He wasn't demanding, just so very meticulous. His mike stand had to be placed on stage only moments before he sang and his guitar was not to be tuned by anyone but him.

They all rather preferred handling their own instruments. They weren't so 'Hollywood' as to be disconnected enough not to care how the equipment was handled. Max had bought his drum set piece by piece over a few years until it was perfectly what he wanted it to be. The moment he sat behind the completed set was a memory he would never forget, and each of them had a similar story. Before he knew it the opening act was starting and he still didn't know if she was there. The set list for the night was long and a bit all over the place but they found a way to get through to rolling applause and crazy screaming fans.

After a two hour show Max tucked his drumsticks into the pocket of his jeans leaving the stage. He'd swap them for a simple practice set and toss those into the crowd, since he wasn't ready to part with the ones she had bought him for Christmas a few years before. They somehow felt lucky, especially because they had survived ten full live shows of none to gentle playing. Drying the sweat from his brow he dumped a cold bottle of water over his head and caught his breath jogging back to his seat behind his drums to play the short encore. He hadn't really wanted to go back out tonight but it was for the hometown fans so he drummed his heart out.

She was a pox on his mind. He'd let her slip through his damn fingers again and he was thoroughly pissed this time. Why was he trying so hard anyway? She'd never want to be with him again now that he was 'famous'. She was tired of living that kind of easy life and he knew she much preferred being settled than all the traveling that he did and though he loved touring it was better when he had a home base. A compromise wouldn't be found in their youth and so they resigned to live separately but he didn't remember agreeing. He was miserable no matter what he did or who. The groupies were endless and each one was more vapid and shallow than the last. They wanted to make him a story they told jealous girlfriends years from then. He'd even met a few that wanted to sleep with all of the brothers which frankly turned his stomach. Those girls were sent away promptly after confessing any such idea, according to the other three it never happened to them.

No one stood out in his mind as the right person to get to know, so he went on with single life forgetting any other way was possible. When the show wrapped up and Max tossed out the sticks he saw the girls who caught them and sent security to invite them backstage. A roadie gave him a towel and a clean shirt to change then handed him a folded ticket and ran off to collect mike stands. Max opened it curiously to see very familiar hand writing.

(*Great show, meet you at Reed's?*)

His throat was bone dry and he tried to swallow without luck. His stomach was in knots and his heart was pounding. She'd shown up herself and made a point to let him know that she was there in a way that would be nearly impossible to fake. Now he was left with how to get past his brothers to go unnoticed. Sure would be nice to see her even if she was untouchable again. It had been a long time for him though it had only been two years in real time the life he lived was hard to keep tabs on.

"Hey Max, are you going?" Martin peeked into the room with a mug of hot tea in his hand.

"Where?" he asked trying to sound innocent.

"A hot red head gave the note to a stagehand, they all read it and shared how very good looking the girl was. Are you going?"

"Can't say it hasn't crossed my mind, you plan on covering for me?" He dried his hair with a towel to stop it from dripping down his neck.

"No need for that, the two of them took those girls you invited back to the bus. You have time, so go." Martin walked away satisfied with his argument and reasoning.

"So go," he repeated to himself, he was excited under the surface but undecided on how he would act when he did see her. He was given a ride, by a roadie named Alex, to his house to pick up his own car. The drive seemed so much longer since he wanted to get there so badly. He found that he wasn't breathing as often as he should which left him dizzy and uncomfortable the whole time. Just when he thought about turning around his tires hit gravel and rocks and he spotted her car parked on the grass with her standing next to it in a skimpy dress and knee high shoes. He took a deep breath opening his door to her smiling at him shyly.

"I was starting to think you weren't going to show up."

"Of course I showed. Your note didn't really leave any other option. How have you been?" He hugged her tightly almost involuntarily.

"Busy, school is hard but I love it." She smiled again as he let her go.

"So you haven't given up on your dreams?"

"Never, it's been my ambition since I was seven." Her eyes were full of questions, "You don't look happy to see me."

"How could I pretend to be when this is very much, the hardest thing I have ever done."

"How's that?"

"I'm leaving here again without you."

"Doesn't have to be that way when we see one another you know?" She slid up her hood to lie back on the windshield and get comfortable.

"Only after high school did we start to feel this way around one another. You and I are connected now so we can't be friends the way we used to be. It's depressing."

"You are the only reason we can't be friends. I just instigated a long term separation," Still speaking as calmly as she could.

"I know it's my fault."

"Max, I'm not placing blame here I just don't want to talk about this."

"Okay, how's Trevor?"

"Unflappable as always, he graduated last year and has been living at home driving my father crazy ever since."

"He doesn't have any plans?" He sat down next to her laying himself back against the cold glass.

"Never, he just wants to live off daddy's money until he dies." Veta's hand touched his accidentally and she pulled it back to her side, "Sorry."

He reached back and linked his fingers with hers, "Not at all, this is much better. I don't feel uncomfortable anymore. You are freezing." He pulled off his jacket to lay it over her bare shoulders.

"I was feeling fine until you got here."

"Does that mean that I make you nervous?"

"Not anymore."

"I'd love to know why that is but I'll settle for why you wanted to see me instead."

"I can't really say. I guess I just wanted to see you away from the hordes of people that follow you around the world." She was still so confused and unable to get together the words she needed to use.

"Could have met at your place or mine, why here?"

"It's a great place to look at the stars." She pointed to the well-lit sky hovering beautifully above them, "They're a little bit closer to here for some reason."

"In as many times as I've been here. I've never looked. You're right though." He turned to see her staring off, asking the sky her questions.

"I always did, at least once every night I was here."

"How many times have you come here?"

"Reed is one of my best friends he lived next door until we were fifteen and then we studied together two nights a week in high school. I must have been out here a thousand times." She was surprised he didn't remember that little fact, though they weren't together back then like they had become after Prom.

"You know, I never could figure out why you knew him so well, makes sense now though." He lifted her hand from the hood. "Why are we here V?"

"Can't I just want to see you?"

"No, you can't. I'm not the one who said we shouldn't see one another or that it was too hard to keep seeing each other and you told me to agree to it and do my best to avoid you."

"Max, I love you and I know you love me too. I just want to be okay again like we used to be." She tried to drop his hand but he wouldn't let go. "What?"

"You just said...did you just say...What?"

"Yes, I love you and..."

"You love me. Couldn't you say that, oh I don't know, a year ago when I asked how you felt, when I asked you to...?"

"I didn't know, I really had no idea how I felt that day. Can't you understand?" He gave up, feeling it was a fight he didn't want to win. He stared searching her face, for what, he didn't know. He leaned into her and wrapped his arms about her putting her as close to him as possible. She smelled so warm and inviting that before he knew it they were locked in a passionate kiss. She fit against him with her hands clutching his shirt, the moment her cold fingers touched his skin he pulled away. "That was an amazing kiss. What brought that on?" Veta touched her lips savoring the taste of him.

"So many girls, every night, are all over me but not a single one of them is you, I don't know them, they think they know me. I needed to kiss you to taste you, to feel you in my arms." He hugged her tight to him again, "You are real to me."

"You are very real to me as well. Let's not do this though someone will get hurt."

"I'm failing to see how that will stop me from kissing you." He pulled her back gently and kissed along her lower lip from one corner to the other, "so soft."

"You are devious, you know that drives me crazy." She kissed him with a peck and pulled away. "I asked you out here simply because you're in town and I wanted to touch base. See for myself if you were okay."

"I am okay. The band is great and we travel a lot. Always busy so I can't think, which makes life a little easier until you invite me out to an empty field where no one can hear you scream." He nibbled on her neck making her eyes roll in her head.

"Are you suggesting I lured you out to the woods?"

"Trevor did say once that you would murder me and tear my head off."

"He was wrong. I've never been a man eater like my sisters are."

He mumbled an agreement into the curve of her collar bone, still kissing her softly.

She could barely stand it anymore, he was moving so slowly, kissing so gently and lingering on her pulse making it spike over and over again. "Max. You are ridiculously sexy."

"Thank you," he slipped a hand up to the exposed skin of her back under his jacket, "You aren't too bad yourself."

"We aren't going to like how this ends." She tried to shrug him off of her. "We've done this too many times."

"Veta, it will never end, can't you see that. We are infinite." Those words took the fight out of her. She wanted to believe him more than she'd ever wanted anything in her life. "We go through these phases and when they are over we sit just like this and work all that time out. We've done a few short rounds and a few long ones but look, here we are." He met her scared eyes. "I'll try not to hurt you this time." brushing her hair aside to kiss her cheek. "We can just be friends tonight but I have to touch you, I have to feel you." Veta couldn't speak. He had left her speechless, there was a tear rolling down her cheek that he wiped away before it could fall. "You can also just tell me to go away if you want to."

"I don't want you to go away at all. It's just a shame you'll only be here for a few more hours." She cuddled into his shoulder smelling his cologne that he seldom wore at all. He was exactly how she had pictured him a hundred times in her mind. He was so warm and shivering all at the same time but he didn't let her go. He was clinging to her just as she clung to him. "Where are we right now?" she kept her eyes closed as she assumed he did as well.

"Sitting on a car at two in the morning," he considered reaching for his phone for the exact time.

"True," why couldn't she look him in the eye, why was she being so...

"What's wrong?" he let her go.

"My head is spinning and I'm pretty sure I am losing my mind right now. You are actually a rock star, how much more attainable does my goal look now."

"Easiest eight years of your life." He followed her so well when she was being backwards, "Are you actually proud of me?"

"Sorry that I wasn't before now. I thought it was incredibly out of reach, but you proved me wrong."

"It was a long shot I'll admit. We are just relatable to people who like good music."

"You know I thought you played some smooth music like you played around school. I guess I don't remember the couple of shows I did come to."

"Nah, we are death metal all the way. We just played around school to get the girls." He winked.

"Using music to get girls is possibly the longest living love story of all time. Funny no one ever does it anymore."

He chuckled at the irony, "Never worked with you, maybe I like the opposite thing a guy should."

"Elaborate please."

"I couldn't win you over with the music. I had to write to you and show you the exact way you inspired some of the words."

"I'm a hard sell sometimes you know." She laughed for the first time all night. She finally felt comfortable enough to joke.

"You are." He kissed her again with hopes she wouldn't fight him off again. Her lips parted drawing him in and driving his senses wild. He didn't have to persuade her anymore she was his just like she should have been all along. She was close to him like he wanted her to be and her hands were clawing up his back. He held onto her hips so she couldn't get away again. He couldn't help but try to taste as much of her as possible, to commit it all to memory again the way he had so few times before. The car made a hood bending crunch and Veta sprung off like a scared cat to check for a dent.

"My dad would be so pissed if I dented the car he may actually kill me."

He got down trying to think of where they should go. "We should sit somewhere else. I have a blanket in the trunk or we could go up to the porch."

"Get your blanket, we can sit on the ground." She remembered Reed saying once that there were security cameras on the house.

"Okay," he hustled over to take it out of the back seat and laid it out flat on the grass. They sat together until the sun rose over the fields of corn in the distance parting with a slow sweet kiss for the road. It was a few hours before he noticed that his jacket was missing, she would take good care of it for him so he let it go.

6.

Six months had given her an ability to see it through the most beautiful rose colored glasses anyone ever imagined. She somehow ended up genuinely happy for him; still she had some very sad moments remembering the good times they had over the many years they played with the idea of being serious. She felt like such an idiot thinking it could have worked out anyway, there was an even amount of time spent apart as together and he never seemed to care when she was or was not his to meddle with.

She swung her legs off the side of the bed and sat up. Why was she so upset? Why was he on her mind at all?

She got out of bed and shuffled off to the shower, catching herself in the mirror with a groan. No sleep was starting to take quite a toll on her face. How was he feeling now? Did he even care about breaking her insignificant heart? He knew she loved him and he betrayed her again, for once she had given over the only thing she ever protected and he'd tossed it back at her like he didn't want to be the one stuck with it when the music stopped. As she showered and dressed her curvy body in soft green scrubs and brushed her teeth. She glanced down at her watch seeing she was twenty minutes late leaving the house. She tugged her long red hair through a rubber band and went into the garage picking her silver BMW for the days commute allowing the drive to clear her mind like it tended to do on a crisp morning.

The hospital entrance was open as she walked up, going straight in to the locker room to check the schedule and see who she'd be working with today. As she walked out she saw. "Dr. Foeman?" and smiled, "How are you this evening?"

"I'm on the last six of a twenty four hour shift, nearly ready to head on home, how about you, young one?"

"I just arrived for my first twenty four, Sir."

"Oh, well you have quite a bit of work ahead of you my dear." He chuckled at the eagerness she expressed. "Good luck."

"Thank you doctor have a nice day off." She went on to the desk reading a couple of her charts and preparing for the day. There weren't any bagels left in the cafeteria and she wasn't sure if she wanted to eat at all anymore. She went into the lounge with just a carton of orange juice to get some coffee. A few other nurses were sitting around looking at charts or thumbing through a book before their official shifts started. Veta decided on taking a seat to shut her eyes for a few minutes.

("Is that really what you want?" she looked up trying her best meet his gaze carefully and not let a tear fall in front of him.

"I don't see how else this is going to work. You have so much school left to finish and this is going to fill all my time for a while." He tried to move a step closer only for her to retreat.

"What should we do about this place?"

"I'll move back in with my brothers for a while to leave you alone. It's very obvious I can't stay here tonight." His hands were in his pockets and he didn't want to look up to see the disappointment on her face.

"I don't care what you do. I'm leaving tonight."

"Veta I didn't want it to be like this. The last thing I ever wanted was to hurt you again."

"Funny cause it seems like you enjoyed it at first."

"I'm not sure what to say anymore, what's going to happen to our friendship or will there even be one?"

"Not a chance. This time it's over Max. I won't come back, I won't forget what happened again and I will not listen to your happy banter about loose band groupies," she replied utterly disgusted by his question. "This wasn't supposed to happen Max, we've been together for four years of me putting up with you being too busy to see me and me being too tired to wait up for you. What am I supposed to do, crawl back to my Father?"

"No, stay here please, I'll leave you the place."

"I can't stay here anymore," she almost whispered. He stood locked on her and he saw her shaking and knew she wasn't listening anymore. She was past it all, over it, so far above. It was a wonder to see that she was still safely planted on the ground. "I have to go, I have to just leave right now." She trudged into her room and took out her purse, her keys and her toiletry bag. She stood in the bathroom going over all she was losing in one fell swoop. She quickly decided none of it was worth coming back to this place. Every item would mirror back what it had seen before and she'd have to rid herself of them either way. Underneath the broken pieces of her heart was the warmest feeling of pride in herself for, as of yet, not collapsing in front of him. She brushed past him to go outside for some fresh air. This garden held so many memories of how hard they once worked together. How everyday was an excuse to make it the best experience for both of them. Never had she suspected that either of their career paths would tear them apart so quickly. Her chest was tight and every breath felt like a chore. She settled on the stone bench she'd ordered just for him last Christmas and kicked herself for not getting a slatted bench with a back. Her arms would prop her well enough to look at the stars and calm herself to drive far away from here and never look back. She closed her eyes as she heard him closing the door gently behind him.

"V, we can't end like this, do you truly believe a friendship, as lengthy as ours can just be clipped this easily?"

"You made me believe we were in all of this together, the band, my school, and this place. You told me over and over how much you loved me for supporting you through this all and it was so impossible to believe but I did. I fought my family and my own reasoning to spend four years watching you work so hard to be everything you so recently became, for **you** to embarrass me yet again. Max, don't ever get caught in my line of sight after tonight or you may find yourself in a tough place to get out of.")

She opened her eyes and clicked her locker closed as she tucked her damp towel into the basket. She lifted her small bag and wondered why it felt heavier after a long twenty-four hours at the hospital. Her keys sounded like they were in the bag but she couldn't feel them. She dropped it back onto the bench and shoved both hands in trying to corner them. When the door swung open, she pulled her wily keys from the inner lining of her duffel. A shadow passed her peripheral vision, she looked up to a man with a smirk on his face. He was devastatingly handsome with his dark brown hair and eyes with a body that looked streamlined under the light blue scrubs he wore.

 "I don't believe we've met, I'm John Parks, the resident heart specialist." He reached out to take her hand in a firm shake that showed her he wasn't intimidated.

"Hi, I'm Veta Iakar, emergency surgeon in training, fifth year med student."

"Let me be the first to welcome you to Mercy. It's a grind." He smiled releasing her hand, "Are you coming or going?"

"On my way out actually, first full day around here was pretty interesting and intense."

"Sure is a fast moving career choice for a med student."

"Just one more challenge along the way. I think I'll do fine."

"Hope I wasn't too forward."

"Not at all, I'm sure it's not every day that a new person walks into the locker room." She glanced down at her watch, "forgive my abruptness, but I need to get home."

"Sure, it was nice meeting you Veta." He smiled as she walked past him.

"Nice meeting you too, I'll see you around John." She peeked at his butt, pleased with what she saw as the door shut behind her.

He let out a long breath, "She was too much."

She pulled the BMW into the driveway behind her father's car and huffed at the prospect of having to talk to him when she realized she wouldn't have to. She fumbled with her keys at the door swearing under her breath as she pushed it open. The house was dark, everyone was at the lake for the summer and she was there by herself thinking about him again and working through another few weeks off of formal school...

She pulled off her work shoes to put on a comfy pair of flip flops and wrestled with herself over whether or not to call him tonight. He wasn't welcome to come back into her life anymore, not after the last time. The band got their own tour, so what if they had a real relationship before that day. Her Dad wasn't trying to bring them down and bing-bang-boom she was on the floor with no one to turn to and nothing to say about it. Oh well, life goes on and it was doing just that. School was amazing and she got to get her hands into real patients and helped them. She was proud of herself for the first time in all her life besides the day she graduated high school and her Dad gave her that Porsche she'd wanted since he began rebuilding it. He had even been there then, helping her clean Mindy for the first time, doing her first oil change and he drove her as the first person besides Veta. But not anymore now she was her own person with no one to worry about except her brother. Five miles later and her mind hadn't quieted yet, what was it going to take?

("Max?" She said looking into the night sky from her bench seat, with a purse at her feet and keys in her lap.

"Yeah?"

"Do you think that if we could do this again we would succeed?" She turned to see his expression of confusion and sadness.

"I can't answer that for you." He shoved his hands into his pockets again kicking a rock.

"We have to stay away from one another again. I don't know how long this time, maybe forever. Right now we don't stand a chance to be happy." She pushed herself up, "I'm going home. Throw my stuff away please, and I meant what I said." She strolled out leaving him feeling dumb struck and very guilty like he deserved to feel in her mind.

Hadn't she always been the one telling him to try as hard as he could every day, for her to be so bitter when his number came in made no sense to him? He sat down; wishing he could toss an arm around her and apologize but he'd stepped in it this time. She may be out of his life forever the only person he could think to call was Trevor.

"Yo, what's up Max?"

"Just sitting here man, look we broke-up again and she left here pretty upset, just a heads up."

"Alright man."

"I'll be M.I.A for a summer tour so take care of her okay?"

"Sure." Trevor hung up and walked downstairs to the main living room, sitting on a chair near the door to await her arrival. He wasn't sure when she would get there so he hunkered down with his phone to play a game. The sunrise through the paper thin blinds bore a hot poker into his cheek and woke him uncomfortably. Every muscle in his body was tight or cramped and his cell phone lay blinking on the floor. He swiped it up and stretched out dialing voicemail.

"Trev, I'm going to the vacation house in Aspen for a while. Don't worry about me I just need a break from everything around there. He swore that it wouldn't matter how far the band made it he would be with me. It was supposed to be us against the world and he dropped his sword for the last time I can take care of myself." She'd hung up then. Trevor listened to the message a couple of times hearing the way her voice got progressively more panicked. He knew how she felt for once, what worried him was her wanting to be alone. A broken heart needs hands to bleed on. This heart was more important because before today he didn't know it could break. He filled a bag with too much underwear and some other things he found lying around his room to start following her to the ski cabin. Every mile had his own heart sinking with her like he was following a trail of pieces he collected all the way there. When he pulled up the curvy, secluded driveway he saw her car and took his first unrestrained breath of the long drive. The Styrofoam cups on the passenger seat were his attempt at a peace offering in return for not being turned back around. He could only hope she was willing to see anyone yet.

The big wooden doors were locked so he hit the bell waiting for a sound inside, it wasn't long before she pulled one open, "What are you doing here?"

"I thought you could use some coffee since I remember cleaning this place out on the trip last year." To his surprise she didn't argue and stepped aside to let him in. "Did you get yourself any food for while you're here?"

"No, I bought four pairs of pajamas and a new toothbrush." She was curled up on the couch back into the pitiful state she must have been in before he arrived.

"I'll go and get some groceries for you later, if I can stay tonight and head back tomorrow."

"I don't care, do whatever you want. I won't be leaving the couch for the rest of the time that I am here."

"How long is that going to be?" He sat at the end with her feet, "so I can get enough non-perishable food to stock the coffee table."

"Would you please forget the food, just the thought of it is making me feel ill."

"Okay, can you tell me what happened?"

"I wasn't important to him anymore and he was ready to toss me aside." There weren't any tears left for her to cry and even her voice sounded dry and course. He wasn't in her life anymore and that was going to be the way it was but Trevor was having trouble making heads or tails of it. "He is still that arrogant, over confident, boy I met all those years ago and even if he retired and didn't have a penny to his name or fame to call on I'd still be his biggest fan."

"But you hate the band." He stood to look around in the kitchen.

"No I didn't, that's just something I said so he wouldn't realize how much I liked it." She threw the blanket off of her, sitting up to really get angry or try to, "He didn't appreciate that at all, I never tried to be a stupid groupie and I was anyway."

"I have got to say you had everyone fooled." The cabinets he was looking through were bare down to powdered milk and some kind of canned fish with the label torn off. "Do you have any suitable clothes to come shopping with me because I have no idea what you eat, are you a mammal or some kind of sloth?"

"Shut up, I told you already that I don't want any food, I won't be here very long anyway."

"Why?" His hopes lifted a bit for her sanity.

"I have to go home, buy new stuff and finish college before I miss my last mid-term."

"He dumped you during mid-terms?"

"Trev please…"

"Just do me a favor and tell me it's the last time you'll do this with him." She shrugged and he could see the tears start to fill her eyes, "He isn't good enough for you, this should have shown you that."

"Would you like to know what this has shown to me? He said in plain English that I'm not good enough for him, if that's the way he feels then I don't want to be with him anymore. Doesn't make it hurt any less or make me want to burn anything or break anything he bought me." She stood up and gathered her blanket and tissues from the long night alone, "The only thing I can say is that I have work to do and I need a place to stay.")

Max was having a harder time than she realized on his half of the country. He was sure there was positively no way she was thinking of him. Apart from showing up at her job there was no way to reach her. Made him want to smash things and scream at the top of his lungs, destroying everything he touched. Damn that girl for always having a slick escape when he wanted nothing more than friendship. She'd never forgive him. It was over and he had an awful lot of things to fill his time. The problem there was with her on his mind, work was harder, slower and even a few song lyrics had suffered in the chaos.

Martin was standing at the door with a strange look on his face that asked, 'What's wrong with you?' "We've got three hours until we head to the arena. Mark wants to do a set list, Matt wants instruments loaded into the van and you should probably get dressed...I don't know just come down."

"On my way," his brother trudged off mumbling some curses he couldn't hear. This wouldn't do. Any other show any other night he would have been outrunning them all with plans and calling the shots. But not tonight on what would have been their anniversary. Max was fading, fast and completely, when she wasn't around to bounce ideas off of or listen to ramble about her serious lust for carnage. Since they met that night seven years ago today, the two of them hadn't spent more than a few weeks without talking. He packed his drums and carried them down to avoid Matt's pissed off ordering tactics that bordered on drill sergeant barks. Mark handed him a written set list for approval, at which he glanced and agreed to. Max didn't care what order things went in for this show as long as he could come back home afterwards and sleep. When he dreamed she was there, sixteen again and giggling about some silly thing or another with her full lips pouting when he didn't get the joke.

He'd see her again if it was the last time he saw her, the guilt would kill him if he didn't apologize.

7.

She'd pulled a splinter the size of a golf tee out of a three year old girl's leg, she had sewn up two separate knife wounds, performed CPR on several unconscious people and watched someone die on the operating table after a close range gun shot. Halloween was a terrifying night to work in the ER, with all the nurses in their animal ear headbands. They tried so hard to make the hospital a bit less gloomy. The very first time she looked at the clock all night she discovered that her shift was over four hours before.

The shower was hot, almost hot enough to relax her but she needed to get some rest before she passed out. There was so much to clear from her mind tonight, wait, she looked at the clock again, this morning she corrected herself. Six in the morning was such a strange time to be getting off of work, no one's fault but her own. She was dressed and walking out of the automatic sliding doors when he spotted her.

"Hey...Veta right?" The well-dressed man stepped out of the shadows to show himself.

"Yeah, and you're John." She tightened her grip on her purse trying to remember what pocket the mace was in.

"I am. Are you heading home?"

"That's the plan, how about you?"

"I checked in on someone who had a bypass surgery recently I was just making a call."

"So are you going home too then?"

"Yes," she smiled thinking the conversation was over and turned away. "Do you have to be home right now?"

"No." The confusion hadn't set in before she saw where this was headed.

"Would you like to go out sometime?"

"I'm going to school and working right now, I don't have time for a boyfriend." She was unconsciously moving away from him.

"I was thinking coffee, you sure move fast."

"I also just got out of a relationship that ended really badly."

"Okay, okay. I get it, you aren't interested. Couldn't you have just said that?"

"I swear it's all true."

"Coffee, we can discuss your busy schedule and how to live around it." He was trying to convince her and it didn't take long.

She twisted her keychain between her nervous fingers trying to think up another excuse that this pushy man would accept, "Okay."

"I'll drive if you want to put your bag in your car."

"Meet you back here in a few minutes." She walked to her car alone trying to think about whether or not she even wanted to humor him and turned around after dropping the duffel in the trunk. "So where are you taking me to have coffee?"

"I thought we'd go to this little bakery down the street, they make a great cup of coffee and these bear claws that are just to die for."

"No food, this isn't a date it's coffee." She tried to make it clear how put off she was about the whole situation in an effort to keep it short. His car was both impressive and oversized mirroring his personality with a gold shine.

The bakery was quaint with a few small tables each with one or two chairs set around them, a glass display counter was lined with fresh donuts and cupcakes and cookies, all manner of delicious confection was right there to taste and buy. She ordered a large black coffee and he did the same trying his best to resist getting that pastry he so badly wanted. She walked to a table near the window and sat crossing her legs. "What should we talk about?"

"How about my life and how to make time, or whatever it was you said."

"That was a line, I pegged you for the serious type and if I made this sound even remotely work related you'd come. Here we are by the way." He smiled smugly sipping at the steaming liquid.

"You lure students to coffee shops often Dr. Parks?"

"Never before today, I have to say though, you are extraordinary. That crimson hair on alabaster skin is a dizzying combination."

"You ask me out and then hit on me? You are the most backwards man I've ever met. It is intriguing to stick around and see what other things you do contradictory to the rest of the world but at the moment I have finals to study for."

"Is that so? You're saucy like a red head too."

"Goodbye." She started to walk out when she remembered he drove. "You can call a cab or anything else but don't walk back to that table."

"Come take a seat for a minute, I won't bite you and if you prefer I won't hit on you either."

"That's not my problem, the issue here is that I said I just got out of a relationship, I'm not even looking for male friends. You picked the wrong girl today, better luck next time." She tried her best not to be snippy about it.

"You are a smart mouth as well, maybe I didn't do so bad. I'll take you back to the hospital after we drink our coffee and since it's hot you should sit down here and talk to me." He sounded so cool and in control with every word possibly gaining more.

"I'll sit but I don't want to talk."

"Pick out a pastry then?"

"Why?"

"To soak up some of the vinegar in you, sweeten you up a bit." He pointed to the case, "Anything you'd like take your pick."

She got a thick wedge of chocolate cheesecake and he got his bear claw, he didn't speak another word until she prompted him. "I'm sorry that I was so rude, I'm very bitter lately and I have no idea how to make that go away and let someone talk to me. You were pretty forward though wouldn't you say?"

"I'm head strong, it's how I became a Doctor and how I intend to stay one until I'm well into my sixties."

"Don't you have a retirement plan?"

"Are you kidding me? I could retire in two years if that's what I wanted to do but I love helping people and I would rather be in that hospital than be at home or anywhere else."

"My Dad's the same way, he started doing Lasik when it became popular and was barely ever home for five or six years I'd say." Maybe he wasn't all bad just because he was another spoiled rich boy.

"The job is pretty demanding but he was always there when it counted right?" he hoped he was starting to get to know her but maybe she was leading him astray.

"He's my Dad it never mattered what day it was when he got home we celebrated like it was a special occasion." She was still picking at the moist cake when he stuck his fork into the side for a bite. She was about to be sick, how was she supposed to eat any more of it? Had he used the fork when he was eating his donut or had he picked it up just to eat a bite of her cake? Did it touch his mouth before or after cake? Oh my God, she wasn't watching she didn't know, her heart was pounding her mind was racing and the tunnel vision was starting too.

"That is really good," he opened his eyes looking at her and saw her hands shaking and her eyes darting in every direction mirroring her mind. "Oh my God, are you okay? Take a deep breath." She listened inhaling slowly in through her nose out through her mouth ten times before feeling a little better.

"Did you have that fork in your mouth?"

"What?"

"Did you put the fork in your mouth before you stuck it into my plate?" she looked him in the eye showing how serious she was.

"No, I don't think I did. I picked up the bear claw with my hands and cleaned them but I didn't use the fork here at all. Is that why you just had that small panic attack?"

"That along with the stress of feeling trapped at a table with some guy who wants to convince me to have sex with him over baked goods."

"I don't want to have sex with you at all, right now I want to check your heart rate." She gave him her wrist out of habit, med school taught her not to fight assistance when it's offered. "I think a few more deep breaths and a ride home will do the trick."

"A ride to my car would be fine. I can get myself home."

"Can I take your word for it and follow you just in case? I'm concerned here, your respiration rate is high, your heart is racing and I think you might black out."

"Do you care about me?"

"You talk to me like I'm no one special, humor me when I invite you for a date disguised as a lecture, and have a mild panic attack in front of me that I caused. I think I may love you."

"Oh no," Veta wanted to laugh at how shrewd a manner he had but it made sense that he wanted to see her home so she let him bring her to her car and follow her to the house. She got out of the car and walked to his window, "Thank you for making sure I got home okay, as you can see plenty of people are here to look after me."

The driveway was lined with high end cars of every color imaginable. An old blue skylark primped up to near new conditions, a couple of brand new sports cars near the door with nice rims and pristine paint jobs. This was the house of a rich man with lots of friends or lots of cars either way John wanted to come in. "How about I walk you to the door? Make sure someone knows about your recent episode."

"No, see you later." She waved him off and went into the house tiptoeing upstairs to avoid breaking up an important meeting between Daddy and the other eye surgeons, he had just arrived home that morning and it was back to business as usual. She didn't know what they talked about but she had no intention of being nosy and getting in the way. Veta didn't share her interlude with anyone, keeping it to herself made it a little less embarrassing.

John called her the next morning hoping to have breakfast with her so she went to let him pay, he picked her up and took her to a nice brunch place with ivy covered lattice work and outdoor seating. "Sure is beautiful out here." She commented sipping her orange juice trying to figure out what she really wanted to eat.

"They have nice gardens and flowers, nothing that smells too much or anything that would affect how you tasted the food. Did you know that restaurants have to think about that kind of stuff?"

"Can't say that I did," John had a wealth of knowledge; he knew little facts about almost anything she could ask and had fun watching her drink it in.

The two of them made progress since their first meeting. He was trying to learn what things to avoid, what foods made it impossible for her to eat even if they never touched what she ate. He had watched her cook and she had allowed him to stay while she cleaned her room once. The joke he made among his physician friends was 'she'll let me into every part of her life but the one I want the most.' John had slipped up by repeating the same line to her professor in a hallway, he was not amused and passed the information along to Borris.

"Sit down." Borris told him one late night after Veta had gone up to bed, "Would you like a drink? He poured a whiskey for himself as John shook his head. "I have been in the medical community for many a year and in that time I have come to know every doctor in town. One of these men happened to bring up my little girl today."

"Oh?" John swallowed hard and regretted turning down the drink offer.

"He said her boyfriend was making lewd jokes about her virtue."

Had there been any moisture in his mouth before it was gone now "It was not supposed to be that way. I meant that I wasn't good enough for..."

"Don't correct me boy, you said she would give you anything except what you want. My colleagues you see do not play the telephone game. What do you want Jonathan? Fill me in?" He may have been seated but Borris was a large looming character with his thick Russian accent, dark hair and eyes that always seemed to look down on you even when he was sitting.

"Yes sir, that's what I said but I meant I wanted to...marry her." John swallowed again hoping her father would believe the obvious lie.

"No, you can continue the courting if you wish but as of now you will never marry my daughter." Shea came into the house slamming doors and stomping up to her room causing Borris to pinch the bridge of his nose to avoid yelling at her, "that one you can have."

"Sir with all due respect, Veta is a smart, driven, quirky girl who makes me look pretty pale in comparison but when and if I want to marry her or she me, we won't look for your approval." This made her father laugh in his unexpectedly merry way.

"Right this moment had she been in the room Veta would have slapped the disrespect you showed off your face. Good luck, get out of my house." John left without another word hoping he wouldn't be banned from the house entirely unable to see his girlfriend, if she was still that anymore. He called her phone to leave a message since he already knew she slept with it turned off.

"Hey, I just made a complete ass of myself in front of your Dad. Call me in the morning?" he couldn't say anything else for fear she already knew about his blunder. As soon as he got home he laid down trying to go to sleep, unable to with his mind racing. A few days later he apologized to her in person and she gave him a second chance but she made sure to tell him that it was a clean slate and the last few weeks of their courtship had been wiped out in the transaction.

Over the next few weeks she realized that he wasn't a bad guy at all, suggestive and funny, he ended up being a good match for her intellectually while still not fulfilling all of her expectations. He was very touchy about Max, the man who made him have to work so hard to get her. She'd ignored a call from him and even that made John incredibly angry. "Why is he calling you? Did you call him? Is he calling you back?" To which she had no answers because she hadn't reached out to him at all she didn't know how he had gotten her new number and she wanted to know herself why he'd called and couldn't for fear of being caught and him being mad at her directly.

"I don't know, I have no idea why he would be calling, we haven't spoken in a couple of months, maybe he's finally wondering if I'm okay."

He took a long moment to breathe, "Don't call him back or lead him on okay. You're my girlfriend now and I would rather not get in a fight with your ex."

"I won't, that bridge is long since burnt, he just had to take a step onto it and see it give way."

"That cryptic, fictional stuff is really strange. I get it this time but you should try talking like a normal person for a change."

"Yeah, I'll get right on that." She left his house when he said that but not because of it, she was on her way to work. Maybe to spite John she called him back, "Hey, you called?"

"There's a party in a month and I thought you might like to come with me. Hi."

"I have a boyfriend, but we are going to the party together a little earlier than everyone else to help Reed set up."

"I will also be helping. Did you say boyfriend? I think I'm hearing things."

"I have a boyfriend Max, and he freaked out a little when you called earlier."

"I know about John, I just want to spend some time talking to you alone. Do you think you can handle that?"

133

"Can't know until we try, see you later." She set the phone down on the seat next to her, he was trying to talk to her for some reason or another and she was going to try but it would not be an effort that went out of her way. She was starting to get used to how even tempered John was and the way he worked with her schedule to spend the most time together. The only time he had gotten upset was earlier that day about Max. She knew she didn't love John though and that had been nagging on her more and more since they were spending so much time together she had little time to figure it out.

She drove to Max's house after she got off a couple of hours earlier than she was due home. They sat in his driveway on the hood of his car which was their habit when together.

"I can't Max, I can't just love you no questions asked, you've been gone for too long this time and I can't and please don't ask me too."

"Veta, I am not asking you to forget what's happened or even to forgive me the only thing I want is you. If that means I get a bitter, angry, grudge holding woman on my arm for the rest of my life I'll take it."

"For the rest of your life, are you out of your mind? We can't get married my father would kill you first."

"I have been out of my mind for five years. We went to high school together and I never once wanted to have anything more until senior year. You were standing by your locker in that long sweater and you looked at me for a second and smiled before going back to your book." He scoffed at himself when he saw her stony face, "The sweater is pale green and it's still in your closet or it was the last time I was over."

"I am so confused right now, you want me you don't want me. I'm still in school and I work at the hospital all the time, nothing has changed I still don't have time for this and neither do you."

"That was harsh."

"You know what I mean, this is exactly why we didn't work out in the first place. The memories are sweet and flattering but this whole thing is getting very old. I've been dating someone from the hospital too."

"What's his full name? I've heard the John or James part." Max's voice was as calm as his mind when he said it.

"Parks, Dr. John Parks."

He was shocked, "Tall guy, square glasses and always wears a small gold cross?"

"Do you know him?"

"Yes and he isn't good enough for you."

"Oh and exactly how would you know what's good enough for me?"

"Look V, he isn't who he seems to be."

"Spare me the details okay Max, I am not a little girl and you or my father will not tell me who I can and cannot date." She stood from her seat on the hood of his car, "I am so tired of all of you trying to control me."

"That is not what I was trying to do, I won't tell you what I heard because it could be a rumor and if something happens I won't say I told you so but remember this moment when I warned you that something is off with John."

"Fine." She walked out of the garage door to wander in the garden that filled the air with sweet magnolia blossom. He stood at the window waiting for her to cool off, she was still so mad at him but he was serious now and he wanted her to take him that way.

Her mind was working too, why would Max say that something was off about John? He'd never stood between her and anyone else had she wanted to date anyone else. It was time to go home and leave Max alone, he reached into the past too often to pluck those heart strings that were his to play she supposed. The path led her straight to the water and she sat down on the dock with her feet in. Max, what couldn't he be to her, he was the mystery man that seduced her in dark corners all over this city. He wasn't half bad at being the romantic either when he planned on getting farther than her front step after a stroll through the park together late at night. He was an amazing song writer and drummer who saw things a little differently than most people. But the worst of all was the way he made her want to change from one thing to another in a feeble attempt to keep up with him.

Why was she agonizing over this? She had a boyfriend who was treating her rather well, who wasn't rushing her into anything or trying to get her to do anything differently than she wanted and just by his track record Max was out of that running. She was supposed to do what was right for her in the long run and being with Max had proven painful twice already. She picked herself up and started back down the path where she saw him watching her from the porch swing. "I've decided once before that there is no reason for us to keep in touch anymore. There isn't a chance of me changing my mind or forgiving you or marrying you, God forbid. I'll be okay and so will you."

"Sounds like a fair deal, I'll see you at the party Veta. We can talk more then, I have a few things to tend to so I'll leave you alone for now." He walked away a bit hurt, she'd never picked anyone over him before but there was a first time for everything. He tried to put it out of his mind and get as much done as he could until he knew he'd see her again. In the next month he lived his life as if she wasn't on the planet anymore. He had even met a girl who he started seeing on a semi-regular basis. The night of the party she was going to a dance recital and couldn't make it so he went with the band and planned to leave as soon as they completed their set.

Veta showed up with the same group she always did plus one he didn't care to see at all, a few friends from school and her boyfriend John. Reed had planned this party with a sort of comedy show and a bit of a concert for everyone. She noticed Max immediately, chatting up a couple of guys and tying down green tarps over the rows of tables to keep out the rain that the clouds overhead promised. She grabbed an armful of folding chairs, placing them along one edge of the closest table to the stage. Wasn't long before he saw her and made a mental note to pull her aside. He had a job to do here and he wasn't going to skirt his work just for a girl no matter how small the venue.

Subconsciously, he watched her walk back and forth from the chair racks to the tables putting each one exactly two inches from the last. He knew she would have some kind of guide and that everyone was in a perfect line as well. She amused him when she was so serious and focused she had yet to notice the dozen or so people keeping their eyes on her either out of curiosity or lust, he couldn't tell. She made quick work of it and left time to have a smoke and touch up her lip gloss before the party started, surprisingly on time. People were arriving in groups and sitting at tables in the same way. Had she planned it the guests would sit in the next seat available at any table and mix so no one was alone. Max snuck up behind her in his silent way and grabbed her hips in anticipation of her jump.

"That's not funny Max, jeez."

"Let's go talk for a while."

"Sure," she calmed down so he let go giving her just enough time to slap his back. "Don't scare me anymore."

"Don't hold me to that."

"MAX!"

"Just come to the car already." He reached out to take her hand but dropped it instantly, he couldn't let her boyfriend see it. She followed keeping pace with him to get out of sight. They sat in the front seat of his car for over an hour talking and joking around, then another hour on the hood talking about how they didn't want to go back, "How long have you been dating John?"

"Just about two months, he's nice." She turned her head subtly to face him. "I didn't know that the two of you were friends."

"I'd say we're acquaintances." He laughed, "Do you think it'll stick?"

"Didn't you hear me, I said he was nice, so no. I give it a few more weeks before my job and my school is too much for him."

He exhaled a huge breath, "Thank goodness, not that I was jealous or anything you know?"

"Of course not, it sure is beautiful out here at night."

He took the hint and dropped the subject, "The country is dark enough for you to see the stars."

She giggled thinking of the last time they were here, "One day, I'll have a limo with a glass ceiling and lay on the seats while I'm driven around."

"That sounds really cool." He wondered to himself if that was possible.

"Do you have any real dreams, besides music I mean?"

"I'm still a fair cook, maybe try opening up a restaurant. Did you pick your specialty yet?"

"I hate that I have to have one at all. Why can't I be the first person to do everything?"

"Sounds like a lot of school," and a lot of money, he thought to himself. "What are you truly most focused on in the human body?"

"I have to say the heart." She clutched her own.

"Do you still want to do surgery or just diagnostics?"

"Surgeon, all the way, passionately, I could never manage a good bedside manner."

"Too moody," He elbowed her prompting her to slide down and stand up.

"Maybe so, I should find my date. Goodnight Max." He slid off to stand in front of her, and reached up to take her face in his hands, slowly he kissed her. She saw stars and heard slow melancholy violin music in her head. Her stomach did a summersault and her heart was beating triple time. His long dark hair fell between them and he pulled back to tuck it behind his ear and smiled hoping to draw her back from the trance she was stuck-in, it worked, she was flustered by the way she'd so easily felt his particular pull. He was exactly what she wanted, was he feeling the same way. He put an easy hand on the small of her back to get her moving. "You shouldn't leave your boyfriend waiting."

"Who cares, he can wait." She stopped and pulled his hand away, "Why did you just kiss me? You seem so concerned about my boyfriend now, where was that...twenty five seconds ago?"

"I wish I could say that was a smart move, but it just felt right." He shrugged his shoulders trying to conceal a guilty smile.

"Look, I'm freaking out here and all you can do is shrug?"

He took her shoulders with a light touch, "You and I are just friends, you have a boyfriend and I am not trying to make you break-up with him over a kiss. I apologize, it will never happen again." He turned and walked back to the noise leaving her alone and dumb founded. She kicked his car and lit a cigarette in frustration.

Never again, huh, we'll see about that little prediction. What the hell just happened, they were supposed to be friends. What possessed him to cross that line to kiss her anyway, however perfect and mind blowing it may have been. She touched her lips with her free hand still feeling the heat. He was so easily swayed when she got touchy but he wasn't supposed to kiss her without her permission. He had been sneaky about it and she was going to call him on it. She stalked back to the party knowing she couldn't take care of it tonight. She found John sitting with her group of friends and explained off her disappearance as a party problem that Reed needed her to deal with. Max's band performed and left the stage. She was picking at the tablecloth and trying to keep from falling asleep listening to John ramble on and on to the man sitting next to him who must have been a doctor of some kind himself. It made sense that Reed would seat them with other intelligent people but it was a shame to her that he hadn't kept the party dry as he told her he would.

She decided after an hour of the endless conversation to speak up, "I am so sorry to interrupt gentlemen but

John and I really do need to get going so he can get to work in the morning."

"She is right, I have a long day ahead of me. It was very nice talking to you Edgar, be sure to give me a call and we'll go hit some balls." They shook hands and he took her back to the car with an arm casually across her shoulders. She was on pins and needles most of the ride home just itching to have a chance to call that arrogant son of a gun out.

John walked into her door and leaned in for a kiss she knew would be lippy and too wet. She ducked it, "I'm not feeling well, maybe we shouldn't kiss tonight." She hugged him and waved as he went upstairs to take a shower. She walked to the backyard hoping Max would still be awake so she could give him a piece of her mind. She dialed his number without looking, one ring...two rings...

"Hello?"

"What is your problem?" she screamed in a whisper covering her mouth to direct it.

"Oh, it's you."

"I'm your problem? Excuse me?"

"No, on the phone it's you. I don't think I have a problem and I don't understand why this is such a big deal. It was just a kiss."

"How are we supposed to be friends now after you made me see fireworks?"

"Stop right there, fireworks?" He asked with a hint of wonder in his peaked voice.

She dropped down on a chair, defeated again by her arch nemesis. "If I could have blocked it, you can bet I would have. That's just not possible to ignore."

"Aren't you dating someone?"

"Yes, I just want to yell at you for making me not want to kiss him."

"I remember someone else told me that he was an awful kisser." He chuckled when she audibly groaned over the line.

"That is not my point," she huffed wishing she knew who he was talking about but she didn't want to ask, "I'm not supposed to know that you aren't anymore. I had forgotten how it felt when you kissed me and now I know again, I have to break up with him...plain and simple, I can't string him along."

"Tell him school is getting really hard to juggle with a relationship." Max chuckled again.

"I save that one for serious relationships, thank you very much...what am I even thinking. You don't want to date me."

"Now that you mention it maybe I don't."

"Oh?"

"I'm kidding. Dump that guy. I've got to get to bed."

"Okay, Night Max." She hung up the phone collecting herself to go back inside and make a glass of water.

"Love you, V."

When she hung up she found herself home with John and wishing he would disappear. He was six foot two and wore his dark brown hair in a shaggy boys cut. He was an artist by night and a Doctor by day. He painted portraits and forms asking Veta many times to be his subject leaving her to wonder just what the canvas would behold. This particular night he'd had too much to drink, which always left him angry and roughly aggressive. Any other night he would have gone home to his own place but since her father was out of town she brought him home to sleep it off knowing he had a shift first thing in the morning. She got up to lock the door and get the glass of water she made; she flipped off a light in the hall and went to her room. He was standing at the end of the bed looking at the floor she didn't see anything and set her drink down to ask, "Are you okay?"

"Why is that guy's number still in your phone?"

"Could you be just a tiny bit more specific?" enraged, he snatched her hair pulling her to the floor. "Let me go!" He slammed her head against the carpet repeatedly trying to knock her out as she kicked screaming for him to let her free.

"You are going to tell me why? Is that who you snuck off with tonight? You are supposed to be mine now you know?" He was screaming through his clenched teeth as she kicked herself loose, standing to hit a button on the wall that alerted the authorities, he grabbed her by the throat with both hands. His eyes were glazed over as he watched her try to struggle she saw a smile start at the corners of his mouth. Veta couldn't breathe or speak or fight him off, he was too strong and too mad, she was hitting him with no reaction and tearing at his hands with her nails, "You were mine, and he can't have you until I'm finished. I'll kill you first."

"Please..." was the last thing she said before everything blacked out around her. A female EMT roused her and checked her vital signs.

"Are you alright there dear?" Veta nodded still trying to figure out what happened and why. The room was brighter then she remembered it being before and her head was pounding. The nice woman was there through the rest of her ordeal helping her through the paperwork for a restraining order and even gathering his things from Veta's house. The police officers put the huge maple door back on the hinges after breaking in to take him down with a couple of tasers.

When they all left she was so alone and uncomfortable that the only person she wanted to see was Max, looking up at the grandfather clock in the foyer she decided to text him and not risk waking him up, "I could use some company if you're awake?" She set the phone down expecting him to be asleep and brushed her hair putting it up in a ponytail, when she came out of the bathroom the phone beeped.

"I could come by, do you want coffee?"

"Yes please :)." A moment later she heard another beep.

"Be there in ten." She picked up the room in an attempt to feel normal once he got there. The house was such an empty place sometimes and with fear in the back of her mind it was hard to be alone. The knock on the broken door brought a whole flood of emotions as she pulled it open for him. He'd brought doughnuts too in a peace offering for crossing the line, the moment he saw her he set them down on the entry table and took her in his arms. "What happened? Did you get robbed?"

"John attacked me." She said through a teary voice.

"Are you serious? Are you okay?" He pulled her from him to check for himself, spotting her bruised neck and arms. He was all knotted up inside and thought for a moment that he might snap. He told her there was something off about that guy but he didn't know that he was violent, what he knew was that he wasn't faithful which now seemed to be a rather foolish thing to be worrying about.

"I'm fine, now. He just kicked me around a little. I don't know what happened. He asked why I still had your number in my phone. I didn't even get a chance to answer. He just jumped on me like a rabid animal." She struggled to say with tears streaming down her face.

"I wish I knew this about him, I feel like I've failed you." He kept her tight to his chest and let her cry until she looked up to him with her red puffy eyes. "Are you…okay?"

She swiped the last tear off her cheek summoning up an almost cheerful smile, "I am now. Sorry if I woke you, who knows how late you were out?"

"You have my permission to call me anytime and if I can get to you I will. You mean a hell of a lot to me." He dropped his hands from her, "You always have."

Veta took a step back, "Coffee, is one special for you or…"

"Both black, enjoy." He reached for a donut to stuff his overly active mouth. He'd never really been in the hero role for anyone and she was the last person he wanted to save. Not because he wasn't willing but because he hoped she wouldn't need saving from the likes of him.

"This is delicious Max. I did hear you; I just can't process that right now. It's been about an hour since a lunatic who said he was in love with me attacked me with intent to kill me. I'm confused and scared, I have no idea what I want to do as far as charges go and I have to tell my Father somehow."

"I know, don't worry about me." He picked up his jacket from the chair.

"Are you leaving already?" she asked a little panicked.

"Only if you want me to," Veta reached out to pull him back against her holding onto him with her fingertips digging into the back of his arms.

"Please don't go. I don't feel safe here alone."

"Then I'm here."

She turned to check the time, "It's five in the morning. That explains why I can't think straight besides the obvious. Could you sleep here with me or do you have plans? It's okay either way really."

He drug a hand through his shiny hair, "I can stay, go ahead up I have to make a call."

"Okay." She took her cup upstairs and climbed into her shower almost before taking her clothes off.

Downstairs he was dialing, it went straight to voice mail. "Hey Carmen, something came up and I can't make it to that launch party, hope you have enough time to find another date, sorry again, Bye." He dialed again, "Hey Matt, I've got an emergency here I'm going to be MIA all day...Yes it was V...No I can't explain myself but I am staying...Cool bro see you later." He turned the phone off and tucked it inside of his jacket hanging it on the back of a tall wooden chair. He'd put on too many clothes for her overly warm house and took off a shirt to hang with the jacket, as he approached the stairs he hesitated at the bottom, 'should I be doing this? She is so vulnerable and scared she said it herself, I can't just leave. Okay Max, get up there and be a good friend not a pervert.' He made his way up; at the top he heard the shower opting to head into her room instead of going in like he really wanted to. Her bed was so soft with the down filled comforter with her fleece blankets that he had a hard time not drifting off without her. Luckily, she was out in a few minutes, toweling her hair and slipping on some socks before lying down. "Don't you want to be a little bit closer?" he teased.

"I don't know. What are you going to do to me?"

"Nothing."

"Just hold me and forget about it all, the past means nothing to me right now."

"Veta I'm not sure this is a good idea."

"It isn't, it happens to be the worst idea I have ever had," she wasn't going to tiptoe around the obvious elephant in the room, "But we'll forget about it soon enough and I won't feel like I'm alone tonight."

"Okay, roll-over." She turned her back to him in the nearly dark room and he slipped an arm around her slender waist, scooting a little closer. "It sure is hard to forget the past when so little has changed about you." He could smell that same lotion lingering on her soft skin along with her favorite shampoo scenting her hair, with the room getting brighter he could see the raspberry lip gloss she wore on the nightstand and her perfume bottle shinning from her vanity table.

"I'm sorry that I like the way I do things."

"Stick with what works is what I always say."

"But?" she yawned.

"Do you have to smell so good?"

"Yes," he could hear the sleep in her voice but she was still listening.

"V?"

"Hmm?"

"That night when you left, I packed all of your things myself and because you never came to get them I put them in a room in my house…not in the boxes but set up around the room like it was yours."

"Mhm."

"It smelled like you. I only left it for a day or two then I packed it up and took it to a storage unit."

"You are a very interesting guy Max." He turned to see Trevor standing at the door. He easily slid out of the bed and left the room following her brother.

"Did she call you too?"

"About what?" Trevor asked with a hint of mistrust.

"John, he attacked her last night."

"Oh that, Dad took care of him already it'll be a long time before he has the opportunity for contact with any woman much less Veta." He winked.

"Are you making some kind of joke?" Max stepped towards him threateningly.

"I'll let you know when I start kidding I promise, so what are you doing here talking about rooms full of her stuff?" That made him step back again and Trevor shrugged off the tension in his shoulders.

"She called me because we saw one another tonight at Reed's place and I guess I was the only person she thought would be awake at four thirty in the morning."

"How in the hell do you keep hearing about his parties?"

"The band was invited."

"Oh yeah, what's the name of that band again."

"Dis-integrated."

"I'm not a fan but some friends are. Were you performing?"

"Look, I'm exhausted can we just get to point where you black mail me for what you heard?"

Trevor was struck by the idea, "I won't pretend like the proposition isn't tempting but I think you wanted her to hear that. Whether she did or not is yet to be seen. If you want to be with her though that may freak her out." He went into the kitchen leaving Max in the hallway after a moment he followed.

"I don't want to be with her right now, I have a girlfriend." He proclaimed feeling a bit guilty for it.

"So why are you here?" he waited a moment for him to answer but he clearly had no intelligent response, "I'll tell you why Max, You are in love with her."

"NO, I mean I'm not in love with her anymore. I'm the one who broke it off three years ago I broke up with her twice."

"And now you regret it," He stated plainly "I'm not asking you to tell me anything but don't you dare step back into that bedroom unless you're here for her. Otherwise her family can take care of her the way we always have."

"Shield her better next time and sick fucks like John won't end up in her house." He tore his jacket from the chair back walking out and slamming the tall door behind him. All of this was their fault how could no one have seen that John was violent? They had all the fancy connections and fat wallets to swing around but somehow this... freak sneaks under the wire. Max was so far past furious he couldn't get his key into the door of his car and threw them into the neighbor's yard when he scratched the paint.

"Are you leaving?" he spun to see Veta a few feet away holding a silk robe closed against her chest, he could see how fragile she felt and couldn't stand to lie to her on top of it.

"V," He let out a slow breath, "I have to tell you something."

"Well then tell me," she waited as he tried to collect his thoughts.

"For the last couple of weeks I've been seeing someone." He said it with his eyes closed but when he opened them she looked unchanged, her eyes were still on him very much the attentive listener as if waiting for more. Those small hands didn't clasp at her robe like he'd imagined they would with the shock.

"Is that all?"

"Yes, her name is Carmen. We met on a video shoot a year ago and ran into one another at a concert."

"Stop, I've been with John for three months and we've been broken up for a long time now." She stepped over to him with her bold green eyes sympathetic to the way he must have felt, "There wasn't any illusion in my head that you were waiting for me."

"But..." Her fingertips touched his lips ever so gently, cold as always.

"Thank you, for coming over and the donuts." She hugged him close to her, "I wouldn't have called anyone else."

"I will be here anytime you call if I can be."

"I know, Goodnight."

"Night," She went back in with his eyes on her, she never reacted quite how he expected her to. She was never truly broken down by him, not for a moment and surely not the way he seemed to.

When she got back into the house Trevor was pouring coffee for himself, "Is he coming back in with you or not?"

"He is not," she sighed, "For once we aren't arguing or dating or friends even, in the conventional sense, we are just two people who live in Chicago."

"How very profound of you," He handed her a coffee mug and pretended to clutch a microphone in his other hand, "You've just won the longest battle of your life, what will you do next?" he tipped his fist comically to her.

"I'm going back to sleep so I can go to work in four hours." She set down the empty mug and went into her room............

In the next few weeks Trevor tried to make her forget about it all but after visiting her on her shift he got a taste of her workload and realized that she didn't have time to worry about anything personal. She had no time to figure out how she felt or how she should feel. She was thrown some of the simplest tasks to fill her time and build experience that would hopefully quicken her response time. He knew she was resilient but how far would she be able to stretch before she just snapped and ended up quitting school to check-in to an asylum. Wouldn't be long now when he'd have to pick her up and set her right again.

8.

Max rubbed his eyes and dropped the pen onto the short wooden table next to the bed in the new house that had finally been finished eight months later then they had been told. He could push out another song or two tonight but he'd much rather go to sleep. His phone was doing something it only did when she was on his mind and he had no idea why she was in there at all. He didn't want to wake her up or call a phone that would ring in a locker either so typing as grammatically correct as he could manage he sent her a cute little message that would make her smile whenever she opened it.

He flipped on the television to check the weather in Colorado while he waited for a response he suspected wouldn't come tonight. The golden haired weather girl was making jokes about winter road conditions when his phone lit up with a happy little chirp.

"I'm sitting in my bed with a glass of wine in one hand and a good book in the other. How are you?"

"What color?" He typed back quickly.

"The wine? White, it's some kind of Zinfandel."

"Long day at the office?"

"Not really, I just wanted to clear my head before I went to sleep. What are you doing up?"

"Hoping to write something but it takes too much work lately. I may have lost my touch."

"Awe, I doubt that's possible, do you need some inspiration?"

His interest was piqued, "Just what do you have in mind?"

"Remember the very first time that we were alone together?"

He really had to think about it, "I do, you wore a black and maroon dress and we went to the movies. Why do you ask?"

"When you dropped me off that night was the first time that you kissed me."

"Oh yeah, I had no idea anymore when that happened."

"I was so surprised and I wanted you to do more."

"You weren't my girl then though."

"No, you hadn't asked me to be your girl."

"I couldn't really decide what I wanted back then but something has changed since then, you'll talk to me."

"We've dated and I know you pretty well now but it's been years since I've seen you."

He hesitated to write a response, "I've seen you a few times, once at a museum with Trevor and the other time you were dancing with your Dad at a wedding."

"Why didn't you say hello?"

"Your father would have killed me right there on the dance floor and gotten away with it as some kind of freak accident. Trevor just looked me in the eye across the crowded gallery and dared me to try but he was right."

"About what?"

"I didn't deserve to talk to you then. We'd just stopped talking."

"Post or pre-star?"

"Post, about eight months into the first tour."

"I have to go to bed soon and if anyone remembers the details of our relationship it's probably me, just saying."

"My point is, I've seen you and I'm still pretty happy with what I saw."

"Looks as usual why didn't I realize that before?" She set down the phone and went to rinse her glass.

"Don't stop talking to me just because of that."

"I'm not, I have to get to sleep since I have two classes in the morning followed by twelve hours at the hospital and I'm dozing off a bit."

"Okay, goodnight V." he plugged in his phone and set it down. Maybe he couldn't have her back like he so confidently thought before the conversation began. Past experience told him that she was far tougher now than before. The old Veta would have demanded to know why he'd seen her at those places, if he'd followed her or if it was a coincidence. He would have to lie and say he had no idea she'd be there and not mention the countless other times he had found out where she would be to show up unannounced and check up on her. Trevor helped once or twice but not the time he had mentioned to her. His own brothers wouldn't even entertain the idea after their second explosive break-up that left Max in such a dark place.

((Matt spent hours drinking with him night after night trying his best to get his mind out of the sad haze that lingered over the long weeks after. Martin set all the gig dates and times Max almost never left his room aside from a show or practice.

The only one who had no interest in Max's melodrama was Martin. He thought the whole thing was ridiculous how broken hearted he was over some girl, the same girl again no less that he said would only come back to do it all once more when she had the time.

 Since Max had waited so long to try and call again he was left without a working number to anyone. He had to call all sorts of people he would have preferred forgetting entirely, just to be told no one had heard from her in a while longer than even he had. She'd vanished out of Chicago for a second time leaving no trail warm enough to follow. He never could figure out why but she always returned with a new car or some expensive piece of jewelry her father bought for her. So he started to hope for her to show up after another few months. He had no way of knowing she had taken the summer off to spend time at the vacation house in Miami with her sisters. All Three of them spent the time sunbathing and drinking the nights away.

Time couldn't have moved slower for him as he waited but the passing time hadn't made him forget to look at the house as they drove to their own, in the street outside was Trevor's beat up Toyota and there he was there picking through the mailbox. "Stop the car man." Max jumped out while it was still moving. "Hey Trev, what's up?"

He turned with an ugly expression of disgust, "I have been in Seattle. I came home early since I think I'm going to die." He covered his mouth before a harsh cough, "Catch you later."

"Is she okay?"

"Later Max, later." He drove through the gate and shut it behind him. Max was completely at a loss for what to make of it. He was sick, true but no news at all. Even Trevor was mad at him this time, how would he make up with him while she wouldn't talk to him. A few days later his phone rang and Trevor laid it out, Veta wasn't going to school for a few weeks but she would not speak to him under any circumstances. According to him, the exact quote was "He is dead and dead men don't speak, at least not to me."

"That girl is constantly putting you in your place." Martin laughed when he recalled the conversation with her brother in more detail than he should have.

"Not as kindly as she used to let me down." Max sat tossing a ball up and catching it.

"Well that is completely insane of her, she only gave you a hundred chances to change the story?" Matt snorted.

"She's not exactly what I'd call the perfect girl anyway Max. Grow up. She was a high school sweetheart." Martin couldn't resist another jab.

"Neither of you guys even know her the way I do, except you Mark."

Mark stood from his seat indignantly, "Leave me out of this shit." He left the room and slammed a door in the distance on his way out of the house.

"Do you see what I mean, she is no good for any of us." Martin thought he had a point.

"I have no idea what his problem is, she isn't as bad as everyone is saying."

Matt took a deep breath, "No Veta is a great girl when you're together. When you break up this band gets nothing done."

"We just stop creatively." Martin agreed with a sigh.

"You have no drive and you're kind of mopey."

"Yeah I know I should just forget about her this time and move on. Hell I was until I saw Trevor."

"He led to the news the she didn't care anymore. She's moving on, so should you bro." Matt patted him on the back.

"True, I'm done then. No more Ylisaveta." He instantly felt a weight drop from his shoulders. "That sounds very good to me right now."

"Fill me in on tomorrow." Matt left the room and Martin went into his own. The house was quiet but Max couldn't do the same for his mind. If she was gone, who would replace her? Why was he still so worried about what she might be up to? The only way he could really move on was to see her one more time and apologize for being so shallow. He never saw all the ways she supported him until he kicked the beam out on his own. Then the outer walls crumbled down to just the raw faction of who he thought he wanted to be without anyone who was interested in who he was anymore away from it all.

He called Trevor back one more time to find out when the rest of the family would arrive. "A week or more I suppose. The trip was winding down when I got sick. She won't accept an apology, I asked."

"I know that, if I see her happy though, I may forgive myself." He felt like he was left grasping at straws, is that what she was trying to do?

"When they get back I'll call you. I don't see what harm or good it will do so I'll let you know."

"Thanks Trev, is she okay, you never did say."

"Sure she's dating another med student named...James or John or something plain like that."

"Good to hear, bye." Max hung up, she was dating someone and he'd let six months slip by without writing a single verse. Closure was a nice thing and he didn't need to see her now that he knew she was doing something else. First thing he needed to do was apologize to his brothers and start getting some songs together for new gigs around town.))

Now she barely spoke to him again but this time he knew exactly why she kept her distance and did the same out of respect. He never should have kissed her that night and he blamed himself for John's insanity as well, but wishing it had never happened wasn't going to do any good. He'd have to be there right in front of her to say it himself.

9.

It never came to a screeching halt for her, luckily being single was comfortable and acceptable for as long as she could keep it that way, she even tried not to think of him and did it successfully because she dove head first into finishing her college years. Every class she patiently wrote notes through each lesson and lecture she could slip into. In her sixth year she began working in an operating room with real patients and even thought of honing a bed side manner, failing miserably. She made the top of every class and attended more surgeries than any other student wanted to, studying hands was one of her favorite things to do. She made fast friends and dated no one, sparing herself romantic connection to anyone the rest of her schooling.

The day of her graduation was the first she'd seen him in two full years and still his eyes on her felt the same even when she couldn't find him in the crowds. She caught a glimpse of him, walking with a happy bounce towards her. "What a surprise, I forgot you would be here today." His face was pleased but shy and even a bit guilty if she had to guess and with him she usually did.

"I figured I would see you today, since Janet told me she keeps in touch with you guys. We're cordial enough." That tap dance in her stomach would never get old when she saw those perfect brown eyes looking so tenderly, his hair was much longer and he was dressed in newer clothes but he was still that same confident borderline arrogant boy she'd known for nearly nine years.

"She never mentions you to me I suppose for good reason. How have you been?"

"Busy, but you knew that." She lifted her arms in the exaggerated black robe.

"Yeah," he scratched his head.

"Don't let me hold you up, I've got to get seated," motioning towards the mass of cloaked men and women filing into rows of chairs in alphabetical order. He nodded and shuffled off onto the upper deck seats. She took the steps to sit in her front row spot ready to speak to the classes rumbling around her, praying silently that his presence wouldn't trip her up today when her father was finally proud of her again, enough so to point her out to strangers just to claim her as his smartest child. When the commencement speaker announced her she stepped up with a gracious smile shaking his hand to take her place behind the podium. "Fellow doctors," the crowd erupted in excited applause, "We've done it. Each of us have completed the long years of sleep deprivation followed by more hours of studying. Now we move on to long years of sleep deprivation followed by more hours of study." She paused for a light chuckle. "We take our first steps to being recognized as an authority on all things strange that our friends are suffering from and I can assure you if you don't already have an ailing friend you will." She checked her notes as the group chuckled again amongst themselves. "We've learned the Latin names and functions of every part of the human body and now we are given the authority to use that knowledge to save lives. Remember that you are trusted and hold yourself to the same standards you would hold your own doctor to...."

To her amazement Max stayed out of sight while she spoke and every word came out just as planned, making that day the very first time she spoke in public. After they all received their diplomas everyone stood around in clutches saying congratulations and giving gifts to the grads. Veta hustled through to get her car and drive towards the restaurant she'd chosen to meet her family, when there he was again, smiling and wiggling his fingers in a discreet greeting. Veta grabbed Trevor by the arm facing away from Max to beg her brother to ask him to stop.

He strolled over casually, "Hey, Max." Trevor shook his hand tightly. "Can we talk for a minute?"

"Sure." He excused himself from his group to take a few steps back.

"Veta would prefer if you would pretend not to notice her. She'll be at Reed's party tonight if you want to talk, just not in front of Borris, alright?"

"Tell her I'll be there," he patted Trevor's shoulder with a seemingly permanent smile on his lips, rejoining his chattering friends who barely noticed he'd left.

Dinner felt so long to her, not knowing what he had said to her brother. She had to stop herself from tapping a foot or a finger and driving her sisters into clobbering her. She'd been picking at her food for more than an hour and Borris was talking about how proud he was of his youngest daughter for doing her best, wishing her well. Once Dad finished eating she dropped her own fork claiming it was time for the party and she didn't want to be late. Shea gave her a suspicious look but with no proof of deceit, decided to forget it and moved to leave herself. As they all dispersed she kissed her father on the cheek and walked out, Trevor followed her to the car sharing that Max wanted to talk. He'd stuttered a bit over the words once he saw the impact they made. "He said he would be there, just like that? He was glad that you would be available." His head hung, not at all pleased with the pain he saw in her face.

"Was he alone or did he have a date?"

"Didn't see anyone with him but I can't be sure. Be careful around him."

"I will," he shut her door and stepped back watching her pull off.

She blared the stereo and pumped herself up all the way there. Reed lived on the outskirts of town now, in the cottage in the country his parents left him when they passed away. She'd known him all her life as a neighbor and a friend since they were both doctors' kids they spent a lot of time together over the years. He was still the laid back red head who skated through med school only ever coming in second to her. The party was in full swing when she pulled onto the property. Noticing Max's little compact car parked near the front of the house made her wonder if he'd come right here after he spoke to Trev. With a confident strut in her six inch heels and thigh length dress she walked into Reed's house to a rousing greeting by everyone standing near the front door. She took a red plastic cup and filled it halfway with foamy beer. This was quickly becoming a loud gathering, luckily the closest neighbor was two miles south so no one held back. Guests had made their way through the house, sitting and standing all around having loud conversations over loud music. The place had changed a lot of the years and none of the furniture she remembered was there. It had all been replaced with modern chairs and glass front cabinets. She was just beginning to feel a headache growing when he took her hand and spun her around into his arms to speak into her ear.

"Hi, can we step outside for a couple of minutes and talk." She nodded feeling that familiar Max dance in her stomach, following him to the back door winding through the crowded room. He held the door for her and pointed to the old porch swing that somehow no one was sitting on. "Would you like to sit is what I meant." He corrected some faux pas he only imagined was present. She sat and folded her hands in her lap taking a deep breath like she was preparing for a verdict to a crime she couldn't for the life of her remember committing. "I need to apologize to you. We ended our friendship very unpleasantly and I've felt bad about this for a long time. Just let me say, I was in denial back then that I couldn't let you hold me back."

"Is that what you thought?" she smirked a little staring at the chipping paint on the wood panels that lined the porch.

"How was I supposed to know what I'd be giving up back then?"

"Do we have to talk about this, I'd much rather know what you're doing now." She couldn't stop thinking back to the last night she'd seen him and she wanted very much to change the subject.

"We have a big following, travel all the time and I get to rock every day."

"That's great," she met his eyes for the first time with a genuine smile, "Do you like being on the road?"

"Sometimes I wouldn't want to be anywhere else and others leave me feeling homesick." He cleared his throat successfully avoiding the home he meant, "How about you?"

"Still trying to find the right place to work, I have to be an intern somewhere before I can do anything."

"What did you end up pursuing?"

"Surgery, heart specialty, I still don't possess the right personality to speak to ailing people I come off cold." She shrugged starting to relax a bit around him.

"I bet I'm the last person you wanted to see tonight."

"No, the last person I want to see tonight is my Dad again. He once said, 'You are always searching for some boy but you need no one.' He was right you know?" she flinched at the hurt she saw, the hurt she wanted to see.

"You don't, you really never needed a guy. I think I need you though, if at the very least to be friends."

"I don't see why we couldn't now, you seem more settled and stable minded. Do you still think that I may hold you back?"

"That's the only thing I regret saying. I was immature, trust me, I never meant that."

"Either way I'd love to know how that's changed." He sat down next to her with his head in his hands.

"You not being a part of my life is seriously distracting, all of my brothers have said that you and I need to settle this feud. They all miss the old Max, or at least that's what they're saying."

"Is this for you or your brothers?"

He looked up with tears in his eyes that never did fall, "I thought this was for us. I really missed you." She touched his hand, "We shouldn't have to stay so distant anymore. We used to be friends."

"I agree fully, I just want to be sure about what you want. We should be friends. You're absolutely right. It's been too long since we've talked."

He lifted her hand to his lips kissing it gently, "Thank you, for letting me steal you away from the fun."

"Wasn't really having any fun, I haven't even seen Reed yet."

"He's been hanging out in the living room, doing breast exams on any girl who will let him."

"Budding gynecologist enjoying himself already," she rolled her eyes imagining how tired he would be of all those parts very soon and priding herself on catching up to him.

"This is feeling more normal." He tightened his grip on her shaking hand.

"Nearly," she replied flashing a carefree smile, "Since it has been so long I have no idea, how are you?"

"The band is raking in the publicity..."

"I didn't ask you that. Any idiot with more than five minutes in front of a TV has seen the ads."

"You meant me then? I'm fine, most of the time, when well distracted. Writing is torture, constantly but I always get something out no matter how I feel about it." He smiled now on the verge of blushing, no one asked about him specifically anymore including reporters.

"That is a nice place to be sometimes. Unsure is a lot less ominous than being positive it's crap."

"See, I know you've said that before to me and yet I didn't remember it without you." That made him wonder just how many things he didn't remember about her and then he started thinking about what could have changed.

"It's not like I said it frequently or anything, frankly I'm pretty shocked that you recall it at all." She had only said that to him once before, the night of his very first paid gig.

"It is a clever little way to be optimistic in your ever so capable way."

"Don't be weird Max, I just forgave you."

"My apologies, how about we go back in and I get you a breast exam from someone who has wanted to touch your breasts since the day they showed up."

"That is a lot less weird, let's go."

10.

After she put out a few more resumes Veta stretched her arms above her head and set down the pen, she wasn't sure just what her next step was while she awaited a response. A few months ago she would have tried her best to relax and enjoy her time off but the thought of quiet time made her anxious anew. There wasn't an escape from her feelings when she had nothing to do but she wasn't planning on having to fill the time until slipping the last legal sized envelope into the mail. She could go to the gym every day and go swimming or she could visit landmarks around the city that she had never seen before, bowling, drawing, hiking or anything. Fight as she may no one could occupy her mind better than work or Max, she'd have to crack open a book to have any hope of getting him out again now that she had brought him into her mind. It was just like him to take over any little thing you gave him even if it was supposed to be a different piece of her mind.

Who did he think he was anyway, some amazing artist, she'd give him that. There were a few times when she caught herself listening to a song on the radio and it turned out to be one of theirs, she even hummed the same song once looking over a chart. She could fight him long enough to get a job offer. She stepped out of her room to look down on the place she was ready to spring from like a prisoner in Alcatraz whose stint was just about up.

Trevor was on a tirade trying to extend his curfew with a passionate argument that had her wondering if he might just get through to Borris, as if there was a chance of that happening. Shea was carrying down an over filled laundry basket to drop on the housekeepers last minute before they were all off for the night. Veta was always so eager to get out of here but here she was, completed eight years of college and only had two failed relationships under her belt. "Don't you have something you should be doing?"

"What?"

"You are standing there with a smug look on your face judging us." Her younger brother cawed up at her.

"I really wasn't...I was thinking about how much I'm going to miss it here once I leave." She smiled strolling down the stairs, "To judge you wouldn't exactly be fair anyway Trevor."

"Oh, because you're so superior to me?"

"No, because I am not one of your peers nor do I hold a candle to the spectacle you make of yourself."

"I'm twenty-four and Dad expects me to be home by ten thirty." His argument would be valid in any other house but arguing with Borris was just a waste of time.

"Move out and you won't have a curfew." She shrugged her shoulder with no other suggestions.

"Ditto," he stomped off to his upstairs room. There wasn't really a smug look or a thought about either of them but stirring Trevor up made her laugh. The only thing on her mind was a need to find something to do to fill her time before she was whisked away into a new job and life for herself. Her Dad would throw a fit and try to reel her in but this time she wouldn't be on the line and there was no way he could get her to change her mind under any circumstances.

The next time her phone rang she was offered a job in Colorado, then Detroit, the offers kept rolling in with mostly local positions with doctors she'd known all of her school years. Being able to turn them down wasn't exactly in her wheel house; they had been sources of study material or quick facts around the bar in this house. Each had put in his two cents and would be looking for a protégé when independence was her only goal. The news would be easier shared if she had a great prospect far enough away to accept...

From her position in the chair she could hear both house lines if they were to ring, the door if someone knocked or rang the bell and she could see the mailbox as soon as that arrived. Three weeks had passed as she waited for something better than Colorado to come along. The last thing she wanted was to follow in Reed's footsteps or anyone else she knew. The postal truck drove up outside and Veta stood straightening her skirt and shirt. This letter was the last one she was waiting for and it was a position in Colorado though she couldn't remember where. The envelope read Denver and she decided it sounded perfect, they were offering a six month contract to take over for a general surgeon, housing was included with his own summer home which maintained a cleaning service. Excitement was within reach and she ran to show Trevor the letter, "They want me to start Monday."

"But it's only six months?"

"Well yes but I can go anywhere once I've completed a residency."

"I'll help you move if I can stay for a week or so after to get away from here." He was slumped down on the chair in his room with a controller in one hand and a cigarette in the other.

"Good, because someone has to drive my new car so I can tow the old one, oh and no smoking in my car so you're going to have to pull over and smoke or quit before the trip."

Trevor smiled happy to hear her answer. "Alright that's fair, time to break it to Dad."

11.

She'd driven five hundred miles, only a little less than half way and the only thing that made the drive bearable was the cd she had made for herself months ago. Max and she were long since over and he was soon to head home from a long tour that had taken him around the world. She wasn't in love with him anymore, not openly, and so she was free to explore whatever life she may choose to lead, so was he. Veta was moving on, not to school this time but to a new career. A new hospital where she wouldn't know any of the doctors as drunken party guests of her father. Living in that house, turned her into the hard person she was finding herself out to be. The years had taken there sweet time to pass leaving her ready to have a place she could truly call her own. One place where she wasn't required to be someone she wasn't, share space with her siblings or share clothes. Her father was so busy with work and patients, they were nearly always left alone to fight it out with Rose, the nanny he'd hired when Trevor started running away. She never had much of a backbone with four of them all screaming and carrying on with their separate complaints. She'd never known anyone less prone to choosing a side then Rose. Funny, young thing her old father had made take care of them all by herself.

On the few occasions she managed to escape the bondage of being a child of a wealthy doctor she found herself thrust into Max's arms. This move would change all of that; she wouldn't need him any more as long as she made friends quickly in Denver. Her brother was set to meet her there in a few days to help her with the unpacking of the ten foot truck she'd driven in, she was regretting allowing him to drive her beamer so long a distance since she knew he tended to speed. She didn't intend to move all of her things from her father's home, but upon starting to pack she couldn't stop until it was all in boxes. Her entire bedroom apartment was emptied followed by a trip to her storage unit to get the furniture she'd bought after Max broke her heart the second time. It was uncalled for, the way he took her dreams and tore them down to bare branches for her to hold. Max was going to make sure she never wished to see him again; he was so abrasively rude she'd even dare say cruel. 'His life was more important than their relationship and the band was going places beyond his wildest dreams, she'd simply hold him back.' Why was that what she remembered, hadn't he apologized and even been there to calm her after she was attacked?

She pulled under the cover of a gas station awning to fill the dusty truck up and check the black car she was towing. It was old scratched and beaten but her first car was reliable, just not enough so to travel so far or else Trevor would have had to. Before she left the house she warned him that if a single scratch was left on her new car during his travels he'd be beaten within an inch of death, to which he rolled with laughter since she was easily half his size. Veta, for what it was worth, was brave enough to dare him and smart enough to find some way of following through. He was her younger brother and for all their lives she wouldn't let him forget the fact.

The receipt wouldn't print from the pump so Veta walked through the double doors to ask the clerk for it, there was no one to be found behind the counter or anywhere else in the store. It was sparsely stocked with chips and drinks stored at room temperature. The whole counter was caked with a layer of filth that must have at one time been dust, a few cats lay in various sunny spots near the windows and the only thing that was clean visibly was the cats' large water bowl. Never dropping the door she turned in a step and left. Forget the damn receipt; it wasn't important anyway that place was post-apocalyptic to the sensitivity she suffered. The best place for her would always be the operating room, possibly the cleanest, tidiest room in the entire world. She kept her house clean enough to eat off of most surfaces, the time she spent doing it was some of the most fun she'd had. The phone was in her ear with Reed or him, she decided from then on to refer to him just like that, talking away about their lives as she scrubbed, polished, mopped, and even waxed. She was a dedicated sister and girlfriend in those days with so much school on her hands that she had to live in the dormitory or the hospital just to be close enough to make good time.

He was working all day and playing music all night which left him with little time to spend with her in any capacity so she took the phone calls anytime they came in. She would play her little role over the phone being seductive and fun but they never got too close or shared too much, almost like they were long distance friends who played around when no one was looking. Neither had any intention of putting a label on where the relationship status truly stood though they both had their definitions within their own minds. One day she'd stop going over all the many ways her life could have gone with him. The fun they could have had or the visits they would have made to all the mutual friends in town when they first got married or the engagement party where they could dance and laugh. Those were all pipe dreams that seemed to leave her feeling sick now that she really thought of them again, maybe she was just hungry. She couldn't remember the last time she ate it must have been a long while judging by the sound of her stomach. Reaching into the glove compartment she pulled out a granola bar to hold her over until she could find a good place to pull over and eat. She was in an open span of road that left much to be desired in way of food or even a place to stay, the road was starting to feel fairly comfortable for her though. She may have missed out on a great job opportunity in not trying out this truck driving thing. The time to think was a blessing she never thought she wanted to enjoy but somehow it made the journey a shorter one.

She was wondering to herself how much farther it would be before she arrived, Colorado was quickly becoming a place of peace for her despite the scare of living alone for the first time. She could feel the stress falling away from her by the mile and all the dashes on the road became a solid line in the dark. Her eyes were focused but Veta was starting to get very tired. She reached onto the dashboard to punch the button on the GPS that told her how many miles were left, happy to see that there was only ten to the address she was given. What would this new place look like with no town around it, she'd taken the place as soon as it was offered and found out that the doctor was retiring to Florida. Not that it was very important what the place did look like she was only hoping that there was a fireplace since it was so cold. The voice on the GPS started directing her to take exits and turns onto dark streets until she sat in the driveway of a small cottage with a pitched roof. The chimney stood up tall and white against the dark stones of the outer wall of the building with its tall trees to shadow it. The neighborhood was clean and spaced out so that it seemed like a grouping of family homes instead of a clutch of strangers. She pulled the keys out of the glove compartment, trying to reason out which one would open the door so she wouldn't have to spend too much time in the snow that stood two feet deep up the door.

Luckily she guessed correctly, pushing the door aside to the dark emptiness of her new home. She spent a few minutes blowing up an air mattress then went to sleep completely exhausted. She heard the doorbell at 3 A.M. getting off of the floor to see who it could possibly be. "Trev," she pulled the door open, "You're a day early. Did you speed in my car?"

"No, I left home early because Dad spent so much extra time after you left trying to convince me that if I didn't drive the car you would have to come back and get it then maybe you would stay home again."

"Well go to sleep, I only got in a few hours ago myself."

"Oh no you don't, you're couch is in five pieces in that truck and this entire place is empty. Where would you like me to sleep, with you on the air mattress?"

"No, tell me you brought coffee for this oh so chipper wake-up call?" She hoped he had but if he hadn't she would just send him out into the world to find some.

"Left it in the car, be right back and we can get started on this mess." He knew if he used that word she'd be even more motivated than before. When he came back in she was adjusting the position of each piece of the furniture in her head to try and figure out how she wanted it all arranged. "How about we get the bulk of the heavy stuff off of the truck and into their rooms?"

"Perfect, I'd rather have that done first too." The night dragged on and on with the massive amount of space she had to fill with all her decorative charms and accents but Trevor was a trooper and never complained no matter how many times she moved items around a room. He hopped in the shower and Veta took out the empty boxes, folding them tightly to save space in the over full can at the curb.

"Hi," a cheery, pink faced woman stood on the opposite side of the street as a car passed between them. "You must be the new neighbor." She approached quickly, her black and white polka dot dress a little too tight for her chest and the buttons spread open as she inhaled.

"Yes ma'am."

"So polite Mishka."

"Excuse me?"

"My own manners would be useful," she tapped her forehead under a voluminous blonde curl, "I'm Olga Shepp. I live next door to your right." She pointed to a small red house sat among a large garden and smiled with anticipation.

"I'm Veta, it's nice to meet you."

"You as well, was that your husband?" she peeked around her trying to get a look.

"Oh no, he's my younger brother. His name is Trevor." No neighbor had ever approached her home before and no one had to be introduced to her back home. She didn't know what to do with her hands or how to treat

202

this obviously kind woman with her over groomed white poodle.

"Alright then dear I see you're busy, I'll let you get on about your business I suppose. Delight meeting you though." She scuttled off towards home with the cute little pooch at her heels.

"You too," Veta called after her with a wave.

When Trevor was finished in the shower he went out to lock the huge truck door, he could hear someone running nearby and turned around to a lovely sight he hadn't expected. Long blonde hair bouncing in a tight pony tail, black compression tank and shorts with the sweetest half smile he'd ever seen. She ran past as he watched every step fall. That was enough for him, he wanted to wait for her to come back around, not that he had any way of knowing she would and with his luck and a few hours of his time she didn't. He was left to try and catch her tomorrow he stood up and turned to go back inside when he heard the footfalls approaching in the distance.

There she was again, slowing down a bit, "Hi," Trevor called out to her.

"Hello, did you just move in there?" she pointed past him to the stout little cottage with its chimney pushing out a steady stream of smoke.

"No, I helped my sister move in though. We're from Chicago but I'll be around for the next few weeks." He was at a loss for what he should really say to her after waiting so long and nearly ended up rambling.

"Sounds like you're close to her then." She wiped a few beads of sweat from her forehead with the back of her hand.

"I think we are, she's older than I am. I'm Trevor by the way."

"Ana, it's nice to meet you Trevor." She took a step towards him to shake his outstretched hand. After a lengthy conversation they found themselves sitting on the curb, she spoke Russian as fluently as he did and for once he could share it with someone outside of family.

She wanted to introduce him to her mom and led the way with very little persuasion.

"Mama, this is Trevor. He is helping his sister move into the house next door." Olga dried her hands on a towel tucked into her waist cinched apron and shook his firmly, "It's nice to meet you…"

"Olga, and you're Trevor I met your sister this morning. Curious thing a young, pretty, woman living alone, it's a good thing she's got you around to help her." She poked him in the chest gently.

"It's my pleasure to help, if I can do anything for you while I'm around don't be shy to ask." He smiled his most charming of smiles.

"Mama and I can take care of ourselves, don't you worry any about us." Ana puffed up protectively.

"What do you do for a living Trevor?"

"I'm an entrepreneur."

"No job?" she tisked at him through her teeth.

"I graduated high school a couple of years ago and I've built two foundations but so far there isn't a desk they can tie me to." He smiled.

"Do you still have any kind of cash flow without a desk?" His cheeks reddened

"I am a trust fund kid but I stay busy on my own." They chatted for a while mostly just Trevor answering her many questions that he assumed he had to answer correctly to be allowed to take Ana out of the house.

"Trust fund, well you're honest." Ana took him back to her room while she changed to go out with him. "We should go out sometime other than for dinner, maybe to a movie?"

"You're cute but we have to get through this one first." The shirt came off as she slipped another over her head, without modesty or concern that he could see her plainly in front of him. "Where are you taking me?"

"I have no idea, I just assumed we would find a place while we strolled around downtown."

"That sounds pretty nice how will we get downtown?" The pants were coming down and he turned his head to preserve her modesty as best he could.

"I'm using one of my sister's cars while I'm here it's her old one that I've been working on when she has had problems with it."

"That sounds perfect." The car got them to the city and she made a point of taking him to a pizza place she liked so he could see that not all pizza was deep dish style. They spent the rest of the night together talking and getting to know one another, nothing was off limits and they spoke in both Russian and English without a thought. He had no idea that he could have found a girl this right for him but she was still just a girl and he had to know her better before he made up his mind on whether or not he was wasting his time.

Another long day at the hospital made her neck sore and tight. She kept hoping that somehow her brother Trevor would be out of the house when she got home.

It was a disaster with him living there the last couple of days. No matter how quickly or thoroughly she cleaned, the moment she left the room it reverted to its previous state making her realize why they always had three maids in the house while growing up.

She unlocked the door to the dark house, flicking a wall switch and found a note from Trevor explaining his absence as a date with the neighbor's daughter. That was sure to go well. Every time she thought that he was beginning to mature he would do something reckless like this. At the least she'd be able to clean the place up. The front of the house was void of any clutter, his room was clean and Veta wondered what was going on. The dishes were all washed and put away, even the ones she checked looked spotless. Could he have possibly cleaned the house like this by himself? The kitchen smelled like her favorite coffee from home. As she poured a cup she heard someone down the hall, figuring the hot liquid was weapon enough, she pursued the assumed intruder.

"Who's here? I have a gun."

A man's voice responded, "No, you don't"

"Who are you?" she pushed the door of her bedroom open to a red head tossing popcorn into his mouth on her bed, "Damn it Reed, Trevor just let you in here?"

"Sure did, like any old riff raff off the streets." He smiled. "Get over here you bean pole, and tell me what the hell you're doing in Colorado."

"You first."

"Trevor and your father asked me to come to check this place out." He answered the next question without it being asked, "You my dear are a princess and like it or not Daddy will always be checking to make sure you are safe." He was at the edge of the bed now with his feet on the floor, "Can I get a hug now or are we too deep into the intrigue?" She threw her arms around him like she had all her life, Reed was the only man her father trusted even when they didn't work out romantically and he was a favorite friend of Trevor as well, "So, why Colorado?"

"The farthest place from home that wanted me," it was the first time she'd said it out loud and she felt freed by it. "It's a nice place."

"So far it is looking pretty amazing. I have to say at this point it's a safe place for you and maybe me as well."

"Do whatever you like. No one is tying you down."

"True," he stood up, "we should get out of your bedroom before Trevor comes back and starts trying to form ridiculous thoughts again." He offered her his hand and she walked with him to the kitchen.

"How about this Ana, does she come back clean?"

"Average college student, pour me a cup," she nodded. "She's on a scholarship but her parents could afford the school without it."

"I don't need to know that much, just whether or not she's a felon or a fake."

"Neither." She handed him a mug with sugar no cream.

"Is this from home?"

"Directly from Daddy who says 'tell that girl to take care of herself, cowboys have guns' He is more than concerned about you." Reed was exhausted but he knew he couldn't stay there, she was the boss's daughter and no matter how close they were it would never be accepted. "I have to be getting myself back to the hotel to get some sleep."

"Can I drive you?"

"That's alright, I can call a cab. They won't take long."

"Just let me take you."

"Fine." He went to the backdoor and tapped his foot feigning impatience.

"Where are you staying?" she asked picking up her keys from the counter top.

"Resort Suites or something to that affect."

"You don't have a room do you?"

"No, not yet, I stayed here last night, which was fine because you weren't here."

"Then you must stay here." She dropped her keys and crossed her arms. "I have two days off and you can spend the whole time with me. It'll be like when we were kids."

He searched his mind for a good reason to say no and came up empty handed. "Ylisaveta you can never tell your father."

"What does he care?"

"That's not important just keep it between us."

"Okay." She had to break this tension. "The third bedroom has a sofa but the one down here is bigger. I can't remember if it opens up or not."

"You invited me but you have no place for me to sleep?"

"You know as well as I do that we are going to be passed out on the couch in the den watching some stupid movie."

"How will I ever live that down if Trevor comes in?"

"Would you prefer to just sleep in my room?"

"With you?"

"I was planning on sleeping in there so, yes."

"That's fine, if you lock the door and he never knows we slept together."

"We've been friends since I was in middle school. We were driven to school together every morning and we sort of dated for a year."

"Relax, I was poking fun at you." He elbowed her. "Are you still single then?"

"That's what I keep being told, doesn't matter to me anymore actually. I prefer it this way." She shrugged.

"Have you called him and just flat out said how miserable you are?" her mouth dropped open, "You can't lie to me so don't be so shocked."

"Right through me," she shrugged again.

"So let's say you told him, what would happen in your warped little mind?" he waited watching her think it through.

"He hangs up, disgusted that I would come calling after how...well he wouldn't be nice about it."

"Can't say that you're right or wrong, at least not until you try."

Veta shook her head slowly, "It's over with Max now, I have a new place and a new life. I think this is a good place for me."

"No more questions, I promise. Let's have coffee and ice cream and watch this awful zombie movie that a friend of mine made."

"Good plan." She rested her head on his shoulder after he put the disk in and they sat there in the midst of terrible acting and strange dialogue, just happy to be near one another again. "Reed, why aren't you with anyone?"

"That story is not worth telling I fear." He swallowed audibly.

"Indulge me?"

"Are you sure you want to know?"

"I've never been more interested in a story in all my life."

"Then I shall tell it, how do I begin?"

"Was there someone?"

"Yes, her name was Daisy. She had slate grey eyes and golden blonde hair that smelled of her namesake. We met in the park one day while I was walking my dog. She stopped to pet him and ask his name. I've never been struck by a woman the way I was that day." He closed his eyes, "I couldn't stop myself from asking her on a date that very moment to which she accepted. We spent the whole night laughing and getting to know one another. She told me about the books she read and how she wanted to see the world and I shared how I loved to travel offering to take her with me. The next five years of my life were perfect, she was this bright light in my day. I proposed to her in a garden in full bloom sometime in the middle of our fifth spring." He sighed.

"You are going to have to make the rest of that up later, I'm so tired."

"Knew it wasn't true all along, huh?"

"Yes, but the story is bound to be a nice one once you finish it." She kissed his cheek, "Third bedroom or with me?"

"I'll stay with you tonight since you asked." She left the room to get dressed for bed and Reed stayed put thinking about how long overdue he was to hold a woman. It made little difference who she was, the action was the same. He wanted to give her enough time to be dressed before he went into the room, but maybe she wanted him to see. He stood up walking towards the open door where shadows were dancing around in the faint light. "Can I come in?"

"Yes," she laughed at his timid voice from her bathroom.

"This is a really nice room."

"Thanks, try the sheets."

"Actually I slept in here last night. Trevor let me stay but insisted on this room." He pulled off his shoes and socks. "Should I leave my shirt on?" Looking up to see a sheer green nighty draped over her leaving very little to the imagination, "Never mind." He tugged it off over his head setting it down on his shoes, "How long have we known one another?"

"A very long time now, I'd say about twenty years or so, why?"

"In all that time I have never seen you like that." He couldn't stop staring at her.

"You had no reason to be in my room after bedtime. You only lived next door."

"How right you are. I always thought you had some kind of zip up footie pajamas or something like that."

"That's because you like to think of me as some innocent little girl."

"We've grown up side by side, you are no little girl." She turned away from him in the bed ready to go to sleep, "Goodnight Ylisaveta, see you in the morning."

"When do you have to leave?"

"Tomorrow afternoon I'll be going back to New York for a while then Chicago to get some things going there in hopes of moving home for good."

"I hope you can, it will be nice to have someone to talk to when I'm home on holidays."

12.

She glided into her well-made musical note bed, hoping the blinds would work for her, Reed had left only a few hours ago and she needed a couple more hours sleep before she had to go back in to work. The ceiling still had sixty center pieces holding tiles together and the light in the room was far too obvious. She stepped out of the bed to pull the curtains and the room was closer to dusk than dawn but still day in any event.

The pillows were too new, the sheets were too bright white on bold black. Everything felt strange, the house was wrong. She could hear Trevor digging through the kitchen and laughing at jokes someone told him over the phone. She was ready to start her new job in her new place and all of her friends were gone as soon as Trevor headed out the next morning. Her phone rang from the bedside table next to her and she reached to answer it, "Hello."

"Hello, am I speaking to Ylisaveta Iakar?"

"Yes...who, may I ask, is this?"

"Ma'am I'm a nurse at Mercy hospital and your father's body was discovered this morning on the driveway of his home. You were listed as his next of kin."

"Yes I am his next of kin...Do you know how he died?" her hands were shaking and sweating threatening to make her drop the slick phone.

"Upon arrival the EMT's said that he was non-responsive and that he had a severe stroke. I'm very sorry for your loss," she said in a gentle tone.

"I'll make arrangements thank you." She hung up, swiped the tears off of her cheeks and sat-up in her bed trying to calm herself. "Tre...Trevor."

"Coming," he said in a sing song voice, pushing open her bedroom door, he meet her heart broken eyes and dropped his apple to the floor rushing to her side, "What happened, are you okay?"

"Dad...he's gone Trev." She sobbed into her hands as he climbed into her tall bed and wrapped her in his arms. He felt nothing, she was an absolute mess and he was fine he should have felt something and he knew that it wasn't right to be so shut down about it but his reaction was simply to pretend it hadn't happened to him and take care of her. "What does this mean, what happens now?"

"I bet you'll know in less than twenty-four hours. He had a plan for this. Don't worry." He patted her shoulder.

She pulled herself together slowly realizing that she now had two tragedies to get over. The job would have to wait if she was going home to take care of her father's final wishes, one of which already came true in her having to go home at all. "Trevor, can we be adults now?"

"I don't think we have much of a choice."

"That's what I thought..." She pulled the pony tail loose and shrugged off his arm, "He sure did screw us over didn't he?"

"He didn't trust us as far as he could throw us. It's a shame he never gave us a chance to grow up before"

"I grew up just fine, you're the one who always fought him so hard. I went to school for ten years, worked half of that time, watched surgeries for hours and never hung on him."

"Did you forget, dated a lunatic and a rock star or did those miss the final cut in the interest of short attention spans?"

"Jerk!" she hopped to the floor and tossed her phone onto the dresser.

"You sure got over that quickly." Trevor smirked.

"Just don't want to focus on that right now. It's over and now we have a ton of plans to set and people to inform. I don't have time to cry." She closed the bathroom door talking to him through it as she washed her face. "Why are you so collected?"

He wondered to himself for a minute, "I don't think he ever really cared about me. I was never good enough for him. Not like Trey was or as smart as Trey or driven as you. I guess I don't feel like I lost anything." He stood up, straightening the bedspread out of habit. "I think we should drink. What do you say?"

"Make it a double." He strolled into the kitchen and found a cold bottle of vodka in the freezer, walking to the dining room to open the cabinet and find shots glasses. He filled them to the top and spun to hand her one. She took it walking to the couch and curling herself into the corner nook.

"Down the hatch." He tipped his head back, dumping it down his throat and dropping to the corner seat on the couch. She took her own shot reaching the glass out to him to watch him refill it.

"Once I'm drunk this won't seem so bad."

"Once I'm drunk, I am going to see Ana to get pity sex." He took a long swig straight from the bottle.

"Thanks for that," downing the second shot she took the bottle from him to take a long pull.

"Sorry, I really like her Veta." He glanced off into nowhere, "She's perfect, I don't deserve to know her." She chugged again trying to douse the fire of grief boiling in her belly.

"Count yourself lucky little brother." A tear rolled slowly down her cheek. "Let's just hope she loves you forever." She twisted the cap back on, setting it on the coffee table snapping Trevor back into the moment.

"Maybe so...What about you, think Daddy's little girl will be okay?"

"One day I won't remember who he was. That's what makes me sad." The door swung open with Ana standing close behind it.

"There you are cutie." She closed the door and skipped to Trevor planting a kiss then plopping down between them. "What's the plan today, besides vodka?" she picked up the bottle pointing it at him.

"Let's go to my room and talk about it." He stood helping her up and leading her ahead of him to wink at Veta who rolled her eyes in disgust.

She stood from the couch once they were gone dialing his number on her phone and stepping out the back door. He didn't answer and his voicemail said they were out of the country. She threw her phone into the street. Collecting her thoughts she walked to pick it back up.

Trevor's room was messy but somehow still clean, the blanket that should have been on his bed was on the clean floor and the sheets were crisp on the mattress. "Do you have something going on?"

"Veta got a call saying that my Dad died sometime this morning."

"Are you alright?" she hugged him.

"I've been better, it's just such a shock. We were there just a few weeks ago packing Veta's things and he was puffed up over the whole thing just like always. It doesn't make any sense."

"Will you be going home for the funeral then?"

"I was going home either way but now I don't expect to be coming back here any time soon." Ana pulled away with a wounded expression on her heart shaped face, "We aren't going to have a chance to come back for a month or more." He said with a touch of confusion in his deep voice.

"What about us, aren't we having a good time together." She said in whispered Russian with her eyes on the floor unable to look at him.

"The next time you come home, give me a call and I'll fly out to see you." He wanted to tip her head up but bent to her line of sight instead and kissed her cheek.

"How can we kiss when your father has just died?"

"Like this," his palms took her cheeks and he tasted her lips that had a thin layer of coconut lip gloss between his own as he tried to forget his sorrows in the subtle flavors of her. He would be back with her as soon as it was possible for him to get away but he didn't want to tell her that for fear that she would wait for him.

"Trevor, tell me what you're thinking about."

"How much I enjoy kissing you," he lied diving back into her possibly for the last time. He'd take his time and draw out the journey over all her peaks and curves until he could read her thoughts with only a touch. He wanted to move slowly enough to imagine her while they were apart, this girl was so much different than anyone he had ever met she couldn't be squandered away like his first girlfriend. Ana was the flower you pruned around to show her off to the world not one you plucked to sit in a vase. If she withered it should be with time and experience instead of being torn away.

The more he thought with his hands busy exploring her slowly the less he wanted to leave even if it was his father's funeral she would be the one he called on if he left now...

14.

Max couldn't take another second of them all arguing, the song lyrics were his and they made it work with great music to accompany but they argued over the smallest chord changes. "That's enough, play it through again how it is and change it later." He counted them off and began, his hands were focused and his foot made the bass do the right beats but he was somewhere else entirely. Max was beginning to really feel something missing in his life. The hottest parties, the biggest shows, girls coming from all angles and still when he got home there wasn't anyone there. Not anymore, the only person he could think of was a nice girl who he couldn't see anymore, well on her way to a new state and a new life away from him. There wasn't much he wouldn't do to just have the friendship they once shared. Hell, the only reason he knew she was moving was Trevor's email, she had ended the situation with John and decided to pack up and move to the mountains of Colorado.

At least that guy was finally out of the picture.

The song stopped, "I think its fine how it is." Martin spouted automatically.

"Agreed," Chimed in the others as they packed up their instruments for the show scheduled the following morning. Premiering it live on television was a privilege none of them had dreamed of to finish a worldwide tour. The last year especially had been a wild ride of publicity both good and bad, though some would argue they're the same thing. A nearly sold out tour across the country leaving them each wanting more, then three months traveling the rest of the world, five years they had been hopping around playing together and gaining steam and now he needed a break, a vacation from it all which was slowly becoming the consensus between the four of them, just a few more weeks. He got into his freshly cleaned car and drove around town to clear his mind, past her house where the lights were on but none of the cars were familiar.

When Max finally got home he went through his basket of mail and found a few personally addressed envelopes to read. The first was a letter from his mom who said happy birthday and sent a thirty five dollar check, he chuckled setting it aside to open the next.

'Max,

Borris Iakar has died.'

Five words put him through his full range of emotions. He was stunned and confused, grieved but somehow lightened, relieved and strongest of all sympathetic to Trevor and Veta. Poor V must have been so heartbroken and lost, the postmark was only two days old but he wasn't sure how soon it had been sent. He debated over calling her and resigned not to because his calling could make her even more upset than she already must be. He decided to go to the bar and clear his head in the dark rumble of the music and clamor of people...

All three girls were lying in Veta's childhood bed. Shea had her head at the opposite end and was tugging a loose string on the comforter.

"How will any of us ever be the same again?" Dalia asked with desperation in her eyes.

"We will all be fine." Veta soothed running her fingers over her eldest sister's hair.

"Maybe you will be but he was still supporting us." Shea whispered mostly to herself.

"I promise both of you that all of that can be figured out later." Veta closed her eyes trying to imagine what Dad would have said as Shea rolled over and sat up.

"Veta? Do you think she forgot he was here or that she ignored him all together?"

"Angel, she wasn't here, she loved Dad as much as any of us and I just know she wouldn't have ignored him." Or at least she hoped she wouldn't, her stepmother may have been young but she was very good to him all the years they'd been married. Shea rolled off the bed pulling a cigarette case out of her pocket and walking to the open window, "I don't know what to think, she knows our whole story."

"So what, why are we worried about that?" Dali spoke up from Veta's shoulder.

"Can you imagine what would happen if people found out? We'd be investigated, all of us."

"That is ridiculous." Veta chuckled, "We were children back then and innocent to boot. We still don't know any details or how it came to be or anything really."

Shea shrugged her shoulders, "Either way I have to get out of here." She lit the cigarette, "This doesn't feel like home right now and I need a drink."

Dalia lifted her head and stood up, "Actually a drink sounds great, where shall we go?"

"Sam's!" The two said together and laughed at the coincidence. Shea ran into the bathroom stripping off her top and checking her make-up. Dalia tightened the strap on her buckled silver sling backs straightening her stockings and short blue dress. Veta got up from the bed unnoticed and walked down the hall tapping on Trevor's door with her fingernails.

"What?" he called from inside.

"We are going to Sam's. Do you want to go with us?"

"No thanks. Have fun girls and for goodness sakes no boys," Trevor called back mocking Dad perfectly. Dalia drove her oversized SUV to the bar at the end of a city block. They wanted to be happy tonight since for the last few days they had been anything but. The air was heavy with the promise of snow as Shea pushed the doors open to country music blaring she looked more Manhattan than backwoods. Luckily the people that were there had no idea who they were except Veta who knew the bar owner, Sam. Dali found a table and cleaned it with a bleach wipe from her purse. Once she wiped down the chairs she offered a seat to Veta.

"When did this start?"

"I save all my paranoia up for bars. These places are dirty." The table was an old stained spool of wire that had been set on its side and topped with glass. The chairs were little more than stools with a short back support to keep a drunk person steady.

"You don't do it anywhere else at all?"

"Nope," she tucked the packet away into her oversized designer bag.

"Three shots of tequila and three cosmos," Shea set the round tray on the table taking her own shot and handing her sisters the other two.

"Who's driving?" Dali asked hoping it wouldn't be her.

"We'll call Trevor." Veta smiled tipping back the shot, it seared her throat. Two shots later Shea was dancing with a tall cowboy who kept calling her 'darlin'. Dali was sleeping in a booth against the wall, first time since Sunday that she had, nearly seventy two hours. Veta was wishing she'd had a drink at home because she couldn't manage to remember Trevor's number. The number she could find was Max, where was he right now? She dialed Trevor's number as it slowly came to her, "come pick us up please sir." She giggled into her phone because it sounded like a drill sergeants marching song in her head.

"Be there in a few minutes, wait, did you guys drive?"

"Yep."

"Be there in a bit then I'll call a cab and drive her car home."

"Smart little brother, we've taught you so well." She patronized a bit then hung up as he whined about having to come but he showed up. When Dalia had gotten Shea and walked her out of the bar, Veta ran to the bathroom. She washed her hands and was headed out when she saw him. He was sitting at a dark table behind a partition, like he was hiding, nursing a beer and jotting song lyrics on a napkin. He hadn't seen her yet and she watched wondering where he was right then. His mind was the one place she never got into and from this angle he looked sad. She made it across the room trying her best not to click too loudly in the tall heels that she regretted shortly after arriving, "Hi."

"Could I get another one of the..." he looked up, stopping his sentence short and completely shocked he stood to pull her into a tight hug.

"Nice to see you too."

"Sorry," he let her go and sat down gesturing for her to join him, "what are you doing here tonight?"

"My Dad died a few days ago, we all wanted to get a drink."

"I heard about that, how are you holding up?" She slipped into the seat next to his.

"Well, Trevor's a bit more upset then us girls. He never thought this would happen, at least not while he still lived at home." Max smelled like whiskey and cigarettes but his hand looked so warm and welcome.

"He saw his Dad in a different way than he was to you."

"Veta are you coming?" Shea called from the door.

"Excuse me," she ran over to explain herself to her sister. "I think I want to stay for a little while, I promise to call a cab home and you call me if I'm not there in the morning."

"Fine," She waved her back in and Trevor pulled off towards home without an inquisition on where she'd be.

The door was lighter than she remembered and even he looked a bit different or just happier than he had been when she spotted him earlier. They sat at that table for hours, talking and laughing like they always did. At closing time Sam deemed them sober and handed over Max's keys but instead of heading home they walked next door for coffee and more conversation. He talked about his band, the long tour they had as a headlining band. How Mark was gaining confidence with all the girls begging to get a little closer to them. Mostly he was interested in her life then, "I'm in a new place in Colorado, with real patients and no one asking me about my dad, which was getting really old."

"I know the feeling. Did your brother see me?"

"Nope and I didn't say why I was staying when I spoke in front of him, Shea is too drunk to recognize you so

I'm sure we got away fine." She looked up to his backlit eyes, "Are you still worried about him?"

"Not worried so much as respectful. He told me to leave you alone and I would prefer if he thought I did." He winked at her over his steaming cup. "So who do you work with?"

"Some great doctors from all around the country, whose names and specialties would slip from your mind faster than the name of some groupie screaming at you in the van."

"You always know how to make stories so romantic," He leaned in dramatically to get his sarcastic point across, "please Veta let's share another great disappointment you have in me, I'd love to see if you have any more." He laughed.

"I don't, your memory sucks is good enough for now, it won't be long before you stall behind your set completely unable to remember how to count off." She laughed as he had a little freak out.

"Do you think that will actually happen, that may be the worst possible thing that could happen?"

"I'm kidding, you never forget your music, its okay."

"Someday maybe, today I need to think about this and see what I can't do to gain a better memory...I could explore old terrain," he touched her hand that sat on the table, "That feels familiar."

"Good to know, it's as far as you're getting. Try and enjoy my hand as well as you can without picking it up, it's temperamental and I'm afraid it may bite." He pulled his back.

"I know that you're still mad at me but it's been a long time now V."

"Don't call me that. You are the only person in the entire world who was too lazy to pronounce a four letter name." She was smiling but she was very serious.

"I thought it was cute, you never mentioned not liking it before."

"I'm not mad at you I'm just sobering up. I have so many responsibilities left to take care of now that Borris is gone. All of my siblings were left with something but it's up to me to figure out who gets what and how they are to receive it. The lawyers have been fighting it out in my dining room every night for a week and I'm so tired."

He thought about it for a moment then decided just what to say, "How about you come crash at our place, then I can drop you off in the morning and no one has to know we were together."

"That sounds pretty good, I don't mind if you call me V. I guess that was just a little more familiar than I thought I was willing to get tonight." He nodded sliding out of the booth they shared to take her hand and walk her to the car. Max, the ever willing gentleman, opened her door to let her get in.

He drove her to his house in the purple people eater that she'd named years before, he kept it running and drove it around town for simple stuff to protect his good cars from bar damage. He pulled up in front of the three story mansion as she dozed on the front seat. "Hey, let's get up to my room and we can talk about how big this house is." She was very tired and her shoes were too much to bear for another minute and he carried her to the front step. They snuck upstairs to his pitch dark room and he led her to the bed, turning around to sleep on the couch near the door. "Do you need any clothes?" She mumbled something that sounded negative so he laid his head down and dozed off to sleep himself he couldn't really fall asleep at first and just as he did, a cold hand touched his chest and he jumped awake startled, it was still dark but he could see her glowing there in front of him. "Are you okay V?"

"Get into the bed with me please, it's scary over there alone in the dark with no idea what's around me." She was so innocent in a way still, she could probably disassemble a person and put them back together but she was scared of the dark.

"Say no more." He hopped up and let her guide him to the tall bed against the wall. She slid over to the middle to let him in being her normal, cute self and he couldn't help but want it to lead to something more. Her back was to him and he curled his arm around her slender waist to put his head on her shoulder blade, "Veta, I love you."

"Love you too Max." she said the words but she was obviously sleeping and much more comfortably as she gripped his arm around her. There again in his arms but this time she didn't smell like she used to. She had traded in her perfume for a new one and her hair was a different length than before though it still smelled like vanilla and almonds.

When he woke her head was sitting on his chest. The entire world fell away when she was in his arms but he wanted to get up and do something special this time, he reached to the tips of his fingers to grab the cell phone off of the bedside table texting the housekeeper Rosalind, who had worked for them for the last few years. "Can you do me a huge favor, its double time pay?"

"What do you need baby."

"I need you to cook breakfast for two. Scrambled eggs, dark roast coffee and bacon slightly chewy and bring it to my room."

"No problem, be there in fifteen minutes." He snuggled back into her satisfied that it would be perfect even if he couldn't cook it himself. She was so warm there against him again where only she felt right plenty of girls had been in his bed but only one ever made it into his heart, not that he ever told her. The first time those words had passed through his lips, to anyone other than his mother, was to Veta and the last time she was asleep. There was a light tap on the door.

"Come in." he said quietly. The door was opened and the maid rolled in a cute little tray with a cloche topped platter. "You are amazing Rosalind thank you."

She mouthed the words, "she's cute," while pointing at V and quietly left the room with a thumbs up.

"Veta, sweetheart, wake up so you can eat your bacon while it's hot." He reached over to lift the top off of the plate putting it onto the table next to the bed. With the wave of his hand he wafted the smell of hot bacon towards her nose.

"Don't tease me, hand me the bacon." She pulled herself up on the bed to reach over him for a piece.

"Works like a charm, I can use that just about any time I need you to wake up."

"Please don't, I like my figure but I love my bacon." He laughed pouring himself a cup of coffee.

"Well eat up, you have to get home before anyone else is awake."

"I don't have to tell them who I was with just drop me off in Mark's hummer."

"Does that mean I get a little more time with you this morning?" he had no idea what to think of such an opportunity.

"Sure just give me a second." She stepped into the hallway outside his bedroom door and called Dalia's phone. "I'm going to hang out with some friends today then head to the law office after noon."

"Okay, try to get this stuff wrapped up we all have to get back to work." She replied half awake and obviously hung-over.

"Will do Sis, thanks," she went back in snapping the phone shut, "You have me all day."

"Oh no, don't tease me please." She sat back on the bed next to him. "What shall we do my dear?"

"Maybe you should bring me home, I'll want to stay right here in this bed all day long fawning over you and how much I've missed you."

"V, we can't just stay here all day or else you'll be very tired."

"I have a meeting at Haufenmauer/Taft at noon so not all day." She winked.

Max had so much on his mind after he dropped her off. He wondered about whether or not he'd hear from her again and how soon. They had gotten along, she didn't mention the break up or anything and he was more than surprised to see how good she looked despite her recent loss she was a freer feeling person in a way. She sure had a way of sticking in his mind long after she left his sight, mostly the light she carried that brightened any dark feeling he had. Any time that he got down on himself about things around shows or some song lyric that didn't work out, she was there to be quiet instead of make suggestions like every other person tried to do. He wouldn't take suggestions or even permit himself to hear them if offered. She could put up with his temperamental moods and varying availability, she fit into all the silly shaped boxes he created in his mind but something always kept him just short of being serious with her. He had wanted her father to like him or at least enough to consent to the relationship. Contrarily, he always got pulled aside and sternly spoken to, usually ending with Max being asked to be more realistic in his choice of girlfriend. Now he was gone and in this reality she loved him, or at least he thought she loved him though he couldn't say honestly. She used to love him, above any other living person and thought of him more than anyone else as well. He read it straight from her eclectic journal that was strewn with comics instead of words and margins filled with poems describing the feeling of the scenes. She was no simple diary keeper and had little in there that wasn't about exactly how she felt. She had seen a spark in him that maybe only she could see. Veta was a sweet girl who asked too much of herself but she had ambition to be exactly what she'd set out to be and nothing would stand in her way, least of all love. Just his luck, she saw him as a road block instead of a leg up, it was his own fault for focusing all his strength on his own dreams. Both of their dreams had come true and as crazy as the odds of that happening were they were no longer dreams at all but reality. There wasn't anything left in the way other than the hundreds of miles. She had to come home sometime or let him move closer to wherever she was going to be.

He pulled into the driveway and went inside to gather his things and head to the studio for the few hours they had scheduled.

15.

"He left them each a few cars or their value as decided by you of course and the trust funds are going to grow a bit but it seems that most of his assets are now yours Mrs. Iakar." The round glasses on his nose made the young lawyer look at least ten years older.

"Miss, I'm not married."

"Pardon me, your father once told me you were engaged, I assumed that now you were married though your name hasn't changed." He peeked over the papers he was reading to give a look of apology.

"Instead I'm the bitter jilted lover."

"Excuse me?"

"How much is my inheritance?"

"It appears to be around two million dollars, a bit more if you sell the house and the rest of his car collection."

"No, it stays just how it is except for the cars he gave my siblings." She cleared her throat and thought things out for what would be best for everyone, "Trevor will maintain the house and grounds, the Seattle house is mine and Shea and Dalia can have his house in Miami. Aspen is going to be sold."

He jotted down her wishes, "Also there is a cottage in Colorado he purchased last summer."

She was struck by the words, "Where in Colorado?"

"Denver, looks like that's your current place of residence."

That sly dog, "Mark it to be decided later." She was laughing hysterically but it must have been inside her head because the lawyer never made a motion like he noticed.

"I'm sure all of you are eager to get back to some kind of normalcy." He stood shaking her hand.

"Yes sir, thank you again." She took her purse and strode out of the office. Rose wasn't getting anything, why would her father do that. Either that or the lawyer had already taken her cut out of the accounts. She wasn't too worried about it since if she had been stiffed Veta was sure to hear about it. All that remained for her to do was clear out the house in Aspen since none of them wanted it. The memories there were too strong and fun since it was the one place their Father actually played. He would ski and tease them all when they fell. He played games with them and turned his pager off for the entire trip, it was the only place he was Dad.

Dalia and Shea were very happy to hear the results of her meeting and left the moment the words left her lips. Trevor didn't care if he got the house or not and he thought they should sell off all of the cars but Veta was firm on keeping a few around for nostalgia. She had to go through his offices and paperwork to make sure there wasn't any other asset around being forgotten or buried among it all.

"Veta, I can't stop thinking about Ana. She isn't like anyone I have ever known and I'm surprised by her all the time." his heels hit the floor and he leaned a bit closer with a softened expression and a bit of confusion, "I think that I'm in love with her. This could be it for me."

"Do you really need to go so far with everything already?"

"Forgive me for not holding myself to the incredibly high standards of self-control that you do. Why haven't you told Max about how you feel?"

"Please don't make this about me, you have only known this girl for two weeks and she was less than pleased when you left."

"We've talked since then, she didn't know what to think about me. She's back in school and she has been sending me these pictures..."

"Stop right there, that is more than I wanted to know in my life."

"Fine, we just have to go back to Denver before she finds someone else."

"We'll see about getting back there as soon as I figure all of this stuff out." She'd spent three whole days trying to sort through all of the paperwork her father kept in his office but the only thing on her mind was staying to spend more time with Max while she could.

"Can I go back?"

"You can do whatever you want to do." Veta reached into her purse and took out her personal credit card. "Fly back and take care to let Olga know that I'm Okay. I'll call the credit card company and get you authorized right now."

"That's okay, I can wait for you. I wouldn't want to just leave you here."

"Would you prefer doing something to help?"

"Name it I'm there."

"Go clear out the Aspen house, all the pictures and food and electronics. We have to get that house emptied and sold as soon as possible."

"I'll get a flight as soon as I can."

"Well," she thought out loud, "Take the credit card anyway, you don't have any valid cards right now."

Trevor let the card land in his palm, "You are doing a great job with all of this pressure."

"Thanks, it's nice for you to say so."

The next morning Trevor flew out, it just happened to be Christmas Eve and his flight was delayed twice before taking off but he still made it there before the snow started to fall. He called Ana to tell her what he was doing and how much he had been thinking about her.

Veta wasn't feeling her happiest on Christmas morning. Her whole family was spread out across the country doing their own things. They had never spent a holiday like this before, even when they were all warring over their parent's imminent divorce they'd managed to have dinner. When she was alone though, in the house especially, he was on her mind more than she would admit to. No one else would answer her calls which left her with his number and a choice. Call him, share a laugh, and remember the funny things that once made her life work or don't call him and spend the next few hours trying to figure out why she didn't. She hit the send button.

"Hello?" a very curious Max answered.

"Hi, what are you doing today?"

"Opening gifts with my family. Aren't you doing the same?"

"I wish. I'm the only one who stayed home this year. This big house is pretty empty."

"Would you be fishing for an invitation or making one of your own?"

Damn he always made her smile, "You are more than welcome to stop by if you want to."

"How about I come and pick you up to enjoy the wonderful meal my Mom made. She'd love to see you." He was already putting on a jacket to go whether she said yes or no.

"As long as no one there thinks it's a date."

"Everyone will know it's a date. I'm on my way." He hung up.

"I'm not dressed, ahhh." She ran to her room at the top of the stairs dragging everything out of the closet without finding an outfit she liked enough to commit to. Why hadn't she brought more things with her? His family was there and every time she saw his mother her heart beat so loud in her chest it almost burst her eardrums. She pulled on a long shirt when she heard the doorbell, "COME IN." she was tossing clothes from the closet when he walked into the room.

"Good evening, need some help here? Looks like a bomb went off."

"I never know what to wear around your family." He pulled a soft green sweater off of a pile on the bed and tossed it at her, he'd seen a few pairs of jeans on the floor but went into the closet hoping for a darker pair.

"Where is your family today?"

"I guess they figured, no Dad no obligation to be here and I sent Trevor to Aspen to empty the house." She dressed in front of him which he pretended not to notice, he regretted thinking that they were so unfamiliar for the last few years, it was like no time had passed at all but she was still not mentioning the sad things between them which worked out well for him too.

"Well, you are always welcome with us." He glanced to the dressing table, "Are those the earrings I got for you in high school?"

She snapped her jeans and looked over at the white gold stud earrings glimmering from her vanity, "Yeah, why?"

"Wear them, they'll be great. Meet you downstairs, heels." He winked and closed the door.

She felt so much better with him there. He was so patient with her and kind not to mention the mutual attraction. Ten years of an on and off relationship had left them both patient and understanding of the other. He didn't want to ruffle feathers and she wasn't ready to call him anything more than a friend.

16.

The house was still just as empty when he brought her to the door, her stomach on the other hand was full and she had at least one more glass of wine then she should have. "Would you like to come in?" the words rolled out of her mouth without a conscious thought.

"As much as I'd like to, my mom might be offended if I didn't get back to hang out before she leaves town." He bent down to kiss her cheek, "How about we get together tomorrow afternoon?" He could see that she wasn't satisfied with the compromise. "Go in and get to sleep, but give me your key." Something in his eyes told her that any question she asked would be a stupid one and she took the silver key from the ring dropping it gently into his palm, she was gone before he looked back up.

The stairs were somehow multiplying under her feet and when she reached the top her bed sucked her in without a moment to spare...she stood in a seemingly endless hallway with doors that were uncountable, each step had her second guessing the last as tiles tumbled to a pit of never ending nothingness beneath. The only thing that kept her moving was the promise of a bright light showing from what could have been the end. None of the doors were open and she tried to figure out if she was moving in search of a goal or just that light. The pattern she had to follow was becoming obvious and nothing was falling away anymore though the tension remained. One door stood open as she stepped up to it, inside sat herself with a baby waiting for someone to come home, she reached in for the brass knob and pulled it shut walking on towards the light. A door on the other side was open so she stood at it to look, a theatre full of fans clapping as she graciously accepted a standing ovation, again she shut the door but noticed that the knob was shinier and newer. The light was even closer maybe within reach when she saw another door, opened just a crack. She took the crystal like knob in her hand and pushed the heavy door aside...She woke with a start.

"Sorry, I thought I was supposed to kiss the sleeping beauty." Max was lying next to her with his carefree smile and without his shirt exposing the tight body she had forgotten was under it.

"How did you get in without waking me?"

He only laughed wrapping an arm around her, "You are still the sweetest thing when you first wake-up, all warm and cuddly and confused. It's intoxicating."

"I was having a dream."

"Was I in it?" he chuckled.

"Not yet, there were a lot of options." She closed her eyes again trying to stay awake now that he was here but the problem with Max was the comfort he gave had her swooning when he was away and sleeping when he was nearby.

"I'm leaving on tour again in a few days, about ten shows over twelve nights."

"Mhm."

"Are we together again?"

"No," she whispered sleepily.

"Can I ever win you over again?" The best he could hope for was a subconscious response but she mumbled something unintelligible and cuddled closer to him, there wasn't anything that could keep him from his dream but she could make him hesitate like nothing else. Who was going to protect her while he was gone?

Who could look out for her while Trevor was clearing out the ski house? Seemed like the roads were closing and it wouldn't be long before there was no way in or out. The tour had to come first because it was so short compared to how long they had been involved. He wouldn't spend any time focused on her and with an answer like she'd given the likeliness of her thinking on him was slim. In four days she would be back in and he would be on the road where he belonged. For now he wanted to hold her close to him for as long as he could and with a little luck he'd forget she wasn't his.

>>>>>>>>>>>>>>>>>>

He was home from the shortest tour of his career and Max felt relieved to step into his own room of the massive house he shared with his brothers. It had never felt so inviting to flop down on the bed with high hopes of staying put he couldn't imagine a scenario that would change his current position. The phone on the table was ringing; he swiped it off, answering without opening his eyes. "Hello."

"Hey, Max?" Trevor thought he recognized his voice, vaguely.

"Speaking..."

"This is Trevor...Veta's brother."

Max was already rolling over to hear better when he figured out who it was, "Forgive me for being blunt, but why would you of all people, be calling me?"

"Right to the point I see. She is coming into your neck of the woods."

"So..." He was feeling more than impatient to end this conversation.

"I wanted to find a place for her to stay. She won't go home. Do you think she'd agree to stay with you?"

He was having a real hard time getting his mind around this, "Sorry, this is her brother, Trevor, the guy who told me that it would be a cold day in hell if I ever saw Veta again?"

"The one and only, would you man? Its three days tops."

"Sure, I can babysit your sister for you. Why not? Oh yeah, we haven't spoken in two years!" as far as he knew and now Max was mad, "How do you imagine this playing out, a happy, friendly hug?"

"She misses you." Trevor hesitated a moment, "She actually told me that she missed you a couple of times. I've never heard her mention any other person that way."

"Give me the details. I'll be there." He answered after an awkward pause there was no sense pretending he didn't want to see her in any event.

When he hung up the phone his room didn't feel the same. It needed a few touches to make it more his own. He wanted art on the walls now; he wanted to put wood in the fireplace and a blanket on the sofa. They also needed a maid to help out Rosalind around the house, no chance his brothers would help him. Least of all for her company, then a thought hit him like a brick to the head. What if she didn't want to see him? There was a distinct possibility that she was still pissed at him. Missing someone didn't translate into really enjoying them in person. He thought about the last time they had seen one another and how he didn't want to leave her house that morning.

To get a call from her little brother though made the thoughts all the more probable, she had his number, the call could have come from her, had she wanted to see him. The bed stood in its place and his head was spinning above it with questions he thought no longer mattered. Never, anymore was she idly on his mind without explanation or in a dream holding his hand through dark mazes. He had left that kind of thought behind when he watched her walk out of their place that night, when he broke her heart. He closed his eyes trying to relax.

((White light shown through torn window curtains on the first floor, he was lying on the sofa chewing on a toothpick when the door opened silently, he was on his feet. Black, dripping ooze was leaking down her legs as she stood nude except for a heavy pair of boots. Neither of them spoke a single word, his hands reaching out to cover her up and protect her from the eyes of curious neighbors. He held her at arm's-length trying to figure out why she was there, in this state or any other. His fingertips felt sticky on her shoulders and he lifted them to feel the black on his hands, it was ink, thick, old stamp ink filling the untied boots to their brims and she was melting into it. When he'd let her go she faded away like a mirage in the desert, only leaving wet shoes to show him she was there at all.))

He woke startled, staring at the ceiling to hold on to as much of the dream as he could. "That would make an awesome music video." That was the third time he could recall having a dream about her that ended with her disappearing one way or another. Maybe it was a message his subconscious was trying to send, he just didn't know what it meant.

Matt knocked on the door as he pushed it open, "You alive in here?"

"Mostly," he rubbed his eyes and tossed back the comforter.

"We are all going to a coffee shop opening or something like that. Did you plan on coming?"

"How late are we?" He jumped out of the bed pulling on a pair of jeans.

 I think it's at noon, so we aren't, get a shower you look like shit." Matt snapped the door shut. His watch said seven. At least he still had time to shower.

The next week went by in a blur of appearances, photo-ops and studio time that would leave so little time to get anything done in his house but that was the irony of living in their home town. He went ahead and asked his assistant to work on it. With the clear picture he gave her there was no chance of it being too bad. He had all but forgotten when he got a call from her for the schedule of his next week and she'd mentioned Veta. He cancelled all but a couple of his commitments to spend more time with her if she wanted to spend time with him at all.

>>>>>>>>>>>>>>>>>>>>>>>>>

((Veta collected her books and crammed them into her messy backpack, the classroom was empty and everyone else was having lunch with their friends and she was grading tests for her biology teacher. She had friends of her own but they were filling student positions as well. She locked the door behind her and walked to her locker replacing the textbooks for later classes.

"Hi," Max's smile could light up an entire hallway in broad daylight.

"Hi, aren't you early?" she stood there replacing the pack on her shoulders and adjusting her glasses with a nervous smile.

"I took the day off..." he checked down both directions of the hall for anyone who'd care, "How about we ditch?"

"Well," she giggled shyly, "yeah, it's only a couple of weeks to graduation no one will miss us."

"Put those books back then and we'll go." He leaned against the lockers in his super smooth way as she pulled off her glasses and slipped them into the case, pocketing her contacts.

"I have my mom's car today actually. She is staying out of town tonight...and if you wanted to hang out at my house we could."

"That would be okay I guess, you got cable?"

"We sort of have everything."

"Cool." He helped her to her feet again and casually threw his arm around her shoulder walking down the hall.

"I'm afraid we're going to get caught."

"We just tell them we're going off campus for lunch and never come back." She started the car and backed out of the spot, the security guard was waving cars threw one at a time and let them through without incident.

"What a rush."

"It really is." His hand was gripping the door handle with white knuckles. "How far is it?"

"Couple of miles." She drove them to her house and pulled the car into the enormous garage. "Here we are." She got out of her side and walked around to his waiting as he takes in the row of shiny new cars.

"This, this is your house?" he rubbed his eyes and stood up to close the car door. "It's not possible." He said in wonder with his eyes locked on the black jag next to him. "I've seen this house before and I thought some mobster owned it or something."

She opened the inside door and stepped in, "I promise you my dad is not a mobster. Are you hungry?"

"No." he followed her dragging his feet with all the blood drained from his face.

"Are you okay? It's just a house and I am not rich okay, my dad is." She leads him through a long hall that led into the grand living room. She sat in the center in the u-shaped brown leather sofa, "Watch some t.v. while I get us couple of drinks." Flipping on the projector she handed him a remote and skipped off to the kitchen.

With a glance at the device in his hand he decided it was far too complicated to fool with. His eyes roamed the room, taking in the high vaulted ceiling and abstract artwork accenting the strange statues that speckled the room. A whole wall was blankly dedicated to the screen the loomed from ceiling to floor. She walked back in with two oranges sodas and hesitated watching him absorb the grandeur her father worked too hard to make obvious.

"It's ridiculous isn't it?" she huffed handing him a bottle.

"I don't recognize this artist, who is it?" he pointed at a long portrait.

"Those were Terrence's, he was my older brother who died when I was nine." She twisted the top off of her drink and plopped on the sofa.

"He was incredible, you look just like you do right now except this," he pointed to the radically blue eyes.

"I wish I knew why he did that, my eyes are alright without being blue." She shrugged sipping. His head turned to stare into her eyes dramatically.

"They are very nice," his lips touched hers just barely, "Those are slightly different but very nice as well."

She shuddered out a breath, "Your eyes are nice too." She said blushing under his scrutiny. He reached up to cup her face and kissed her with a feather light touch. Her shoulders went lax, the kiss turned steamy and each little peck drew her into him, he let his hands slip down to her shoulders and felt her shaking.

"Should I stop?" she shook her head no and tugged his shirt to kiss him again.))

Her eyes popped open as the dream faded from her mind, she sat up untangling the blankets from her legs. What kind of dream was that, she hadn't seen Max in that way for a long time and he had never kissed her in the house and it was only a week before the conference in Chicago that would bring her home a second time since moving away. She didn't even want to think of what that could mean and decided to let the entire thing go.

17.

He packed his drums, the one way he felt he stayed grounded unlike all those other "stars" that just floated away and it was a nice way to stay sane. Max was determined to stay out here a long time, chasing the dream he'd had since he was a fifteen year old boy with a cheap drum set his uncle bought him for Christmas. The day they discovered how talented the four of them really were when they all began playing within months of receiving instruments. Perhaps his uncle had a sense for what they'd be good at and made it happen no matter what anyone else said.

The only thing missing was that person, the one who would make home all the more inviting and the road more bearable and unbearable as well. Until recently that was just a silhouette with no face, getting less visible all the time, then one day the sun came out and the eyes were so familiar, he swore to himself at just the memory of the revelation. He thought about how it came to him that day, in the studio, Martin's voice filling the overheads with his melancholy ballad of love in fire. Her image jumped into his mind nearly taking his feet out from beneath him. That's when he knew it would never be okay again without her. The next few weeks were filled with shows and interviews he couldn't get out of. He was left with trying to call her or maybe write her a letter spelling out all the beautiful ways he wished she was his. She would need convincing better than and so he waited and the opportunity fell in his lap when Trevor called the day the last tour ended. She was speaking at a conference and needed a place to stay because she didn't want to stay in that empty house. Trevor thought it was better she stay with a friend than in some hotel full of single male doctors all alone. Max agreed and decided to tell Trevor his plan to which he replied, "Good luck there buddy," and meant that he had absolutely no chance.

Trevor didn't know her as well as he did though and Max thought that him saying so made it all the more possible.

The rest was up to him, he thanked his lucky stars that she could come at all, much less stay in his house and possibly take him back. Veta was worth the wait and the extra work. She wouldn't resent him for his late nights or long weekends. Veta would hop a plane cross country just to spend a day with him.

The last cymbal was taken apart and wrapped in its velveteen rag to be stored with the rest of his drums, he was ready to go down to the bus until his phone vibrated against his thigh. He pulled it out and opened the message.

"Heading to bed, wanted to say goodnight. Hope the show was awesome."

"Just got finished it was great. Do you have to go to bed just now?" he lifted a case to carry it to the van when his phone rang.

"No, I can talk a minute."

He laughed, her favorite sound, "Why did you send me goodnight then?" He set down the drum and started to wander around the stage a bit.

"Thought you were still rocking it out and I didn't want you to feel obligated to text me back."

"Oh, I could never feel pressured to talk to you. You're so modest sometimes."

"How's that?"

"You don't want to bother me, when did that start? Just a few years ago you would complain when I wouldn't answer a message during a show."

"Well, now you're actually signed and required to do those shows and we aren't dating."

"I'm seeing the distinction now." He leaned against a speaker amused by the change.

"Are you mad?" She bit her bottom lip.

"Nah that stuff is in the past anyway, how was your night?"

"Very long hours at work ending in an uncomfortable conversation with Trevor about whether or not I am seeing anyone, as if I would tell him that."

"So tell me, are you seeing anyone?"

"I wouldn't tell you either way, if I was dating someone you would be jealous and if I'm not you'll feel pity for me and to be honest I'm not open to either at the moment."

"Tell me then, what would you like me to feel for you?" She could hear that he was smiling and wondered if it was a sarcastic smile or some way of him being sly.

"You're my friend I want you to be happy for me."

"Your friend, I am that aren't I?"

"We've made love in the last couple of months but you weren't serious about all that stuff."

"Excuse me, I told you how serious I was about that and I won't have you downplay this, I just want to know if we are allowed to date other people? What would you prefer?"

"Keep it in your pants rock star." She smiled when she heard him scoff on the other end.

"Consider it done, you do the same. Keep it in pants."

"Sounds good," Veta yawned, "I'm really tired, I think I have to go to bed after all."

He groaned jokingly, "Okay I guess, goodnight V."

"Goodnight Max." When she hung up the phone he started to wonder whether or not she was going to be at a conference there since she had yet to mention it. Trevor had given him flight numbers and times but she hadn't even said she was going to be in Chicago, would she keep it from him just to avoid him? He doubted that possibility since she had just said not to be with anyone else yet something was nagging him still. If she had wanted to stay with him wouldn't she have said so?

18.

She stood in the doorway at the baggage claim debating on whether or not to call a cab when her phone rang in her pocket. "Hello."

"Hi, I heard you were heading into town. When do you arrive?"

"You're already here aren't you?"

"Just about to pull up so grab that little green bag at your feet and get the luggage to the curb for me."

She laughed hanging up the phone and pulling the two small bags out to his new gold car. He stepped out and put her bags into the back seat and opened the door for her, "My lady." She sat in the car as he hustled around to his own side, "So, where to?"

"I don't have reservations anywhere, I guess I was hoping to pop in on a friend and see if I could stay over." She said grinning back at him.

"What friend would you like me to drop you off to then?" She playfully slapped his arm, "Ouch, I was kidding. If I don't get a bruise there I'll be surprised."

"I'm sorry then, you're okay or should I begin the amputation?"

He reached over linking his fingers with hers to lift them to his lips. "I missed you kid."

"Feelings mutual," Her cheeks flushed, "I can stay with you right, because the reservations thing was serious."

"Of course, you are always welcome at Casa Max."

"How did you know I was coming?"

"I would tell you but I don't think you'll believe me." He wiggled his eyebrows to the tune of the mysterious music only he heard.

"Please….." She gave him her best pouting face to which he always conceded.

"Okay, okay put away the big guns. It was Trev. He called to see if I was in town and casually mentioned you and your flight number." He rattled off giving her sidelong glances.

"Trevor? You were right, I don't believe you." She cleared her throat turning back to him, "Did he tell you to watch me?"

"Not in those words, no," He glanced at her to assure his truth, "he said you needed a place to stay, a safe place."

"My brother is a killjoy. Don't keep me too safe."

His car pulled into the driveway past the steel gates and turned off the engine. "Here we are."

"I suppose so," she peered out the windshield trying to find the top she couldn't remember really looking at the house the last time she was there. "Does one man need so much real-estate?"

"We never have less than five people living here at a time."

A smile spread across her cheeks, "Your brothers live here, don't they? I thought everyone was just in town for the holiday but they live here."

"They do in fact, all three of them." He popped open his door, "You ready for this, you're sure?"

She opened her door and almost ran up the stairs, "Come unlock this door, come on." while tapping her foot impatiently. He strolled, teasing her a bit since she looked so excited he'd always said she looked cute when she was excited. He looked at each of the keys on the ring, studying them like he had no idea which one worked.

"Are you kidding me?"

"Obviously." He pushed the doors apart with no key at all. There in the foyer sat three nearly exact copies of Max. Matt was the youngest and still chose to wear his personality on his face in the form of several piercings. Mark was the third; he always wore a short military cut, he was the one who also set the shows. The oldest was Martin and everywhere he went a guitar was sure to follow. As Max slammed the door shut they all snapped around spotting Veta at the door. Mark hopped the couch to swipe her up in a big bear hug, "How have you been?" setting her down again.

"I'm great," Matt hugged her next, "I had no idea you were here."

"Well where else would we be? It's not like because we make it big we aren't going to still be the same people." Martin said scowling from his seat on the ottoman.

"He's such a downer Veta, Fix him." Matt begged with clasped hands.

Martin rolled his eyes, "There is nothing wrong with me at all, you are all just too happy to invite this, girl into the house."

"That reminds me; I stopped at the duty free shop in the airport and got this pack of gum. Do you know anyone who would like it?" She tossed the silver pack at him. "I was thinking about just leaving it here."

He flipped it over and read the label finally cracking a smile. "You remember everything." He strolled reluctantly over to give her a casual hug.

"Only stuff that matters." Max stepped up behind her, breaking up the love fest.

"I'll show you to my room." His brothers all grumbled as he led her up the stairs then to the right down a long hallway covered in posters. He stopped at a shiny black door that opened to a huge bedroom suite. The walls were painted in a marbled black and gold with ten foot ceilings topped with gold molding with fleur de les patterns along with ivy. The furniture was gold studded black leather, a four poster gothic bed made in the same colors as the room a set of couches and a reclining chair. She stood in awe at the door, taking in the grand bachelor pad, dark wood floors and thick rugs as well as a counter that lined a wall. She saw him in all the details down to the cow skull that was spray painted gold and hung on the wall above the bed. He was a rock star after all, not the gig scraping boy she'd known so well once.

"You've done well for yourself."

"I am comfortable I'd say." He put her bags into the closet. "You get to stay in here. I can sleep on the sofa, up here or downstairs."

"You don't have any other rooms?"

"Of course we do but if I stay there, everyone will know I struck out." He chuckled. "I can stay in another room I guess."

"I meant for me."

"No way, you get the best room in the house. Plus they are less likely to try and steal you from my room."

"Do you truly believe any of them would try, after all of our history?" She sat on the chest at the foot of his bed, crossing her legs slowly.

"They've been known to do worse." He averted his eyes trying to keep a hold of his train of thought. "The bathroom is to the left, the third switch on the wall turns on the shower...um, how long are you staying?"

"A few days at the most."

"Oh, that's all huh?" he rubbed the back of his neck.

"Yep, just want to get through this conference and get back to my job."

"V, are you okay? I haven't seen you since your father died and I've been worried."

"I'm good. Can't really jump up and down and change it, so I'm coping." She brushed a stray tear off of her cheek.

"Would you like a drink?"

"I thought you'd never ask. Scotch on the rocks." He pulled open the door of a cabinet bar and poured the drinks, dropping in ice cubes from the bucket on top. "I've always got alcohol handy. One of those perks of being a celebrity," Handing her the square crystal glass.

"Max, I think you may be an alcoholic."

"Ditto." He clinked glasses with her.

"Ah, okay I drink but not very often."

"You've only been gone for six months and all the sudden this happens dragging you back kicking and screaming. I'd drink too." He sat at her side and she put her head on his shoulder.

"I'm so tired. The woman next to me on the plane talked the entire flight." She did a yapping motion with her hand.

"I hate those people; I don't care about your grandkids or your lapdog, shut up." She giggled at him, "Put your damn pictures away." She poked him in the side.

"Stop it, she was sweet, just a little unwelcome after a full day's shift."

"I am sure she was." He put an arm around her to pull her up and walk her to the bed. She climbed in over the blankets to the far side and he slid in next to her. Her head on his chest was the most comfortable she'd been in a while and she let out a long cozy sigh he recognized. "This is the life isn't it, a big comfy bed to sleep in the middle of the day?"

"It really is." She drifted off remembering the first time she had met him. The very little she remembered of it.

Her eyes opened to the door of the room and his arm was draped around her waist. She slipped her hand under his linking her fingers tightly. With a quick tug from him she was on top of him. "Good morning." He kissed her cheek and chuckled. "You sleep so heavily, I could have marched the whole world through here and you wouldn't have even blinked."

"It's a learned skill from having to sleep in so many noisy places." She cuddled into his chest sighing and stretching, "Is it morning yet?"

"For a few hours now, I closed my blackout curtains so it would stay dark." He reached out for the sleek black remote and set the curtains on a slow retreat to their spaces in the sills. The room lightened up more by the moment.

"Now, that's more like it." She sat up and stretched again smelling coffee and thinking she's finally going crazy. He slid out of bed pulling a white shirt over his head, walking across the room to the alcohol stand he'd opened before. He took out a coffee cup and came back to a silver serving station at his side of the bed.

"Rosalind brought this in earlier but I asked her to forget the second mug so we didn't wake you." He started to pour her a cup then stopped. "Are you taking anything new in your coffee?"

"Same old, same old," He handed her the dangerously full mug. "Perfect, thank you."

"I have a cup every morning, usually made by myself, but my brothers thought we would be naked."

"What's funnier than an unsuspecting maid walking in on debauchery?" She giggled slipping her feet into her high heeled shoes.

"Please tell me you brought another pair of shoes without spikes on the bottom of them."

"And what if I didn't?" She looked at him suspiciously.

"I won't take you to the House in stilettos."

"Who says I want to go to some dusty old warehouse anyway?"

"Don't say that you don't care about the huge party they are throwing for the holidays?"

"Hopefully I won't be able to attend."

He stared at her for a moment trying to form words. "You are making a joke right now right?"

"I have shoes for any occasion but right now I have to go and get ready to go to the conference and try to stay awake and look interested, as I announce three hours' worth of lecturers." She unzipped her carry-on bag pulling out her toiletries and a pale colored sundress. "Which one is the bathroom again?"

He pointed straight behind her, she pushed the door open fumbling for a light switch. The teal and forest green walls caught her off guard and as she turned slowly to see the rest. The shower head hung in the center of the room with a bed of smooth rocks to stand on. The bath tub had a waterfall that seemed to come in from outside. It was a beautiful tropical paradise right down to the potted pygmy palm trees and elephant plants.

His head poked in the door, "The third switch on the wall is the shower and its set at ninety nine degrees."

"Where is the curtain?" She looked at him shyly over her shoulder.

"There isn't one. You just have to stand in the room and trust me not to open the door."

"I am not worried about you."

"I'll go and entertain them, its band practice anyway." He kissed her on the cheek. "Here are the keys to the house, the room, and the black car in the driveway. Make yourself at home." He winked handing her the key ring, "I trust you."

"Thanks." Once he was gone she weighed the keys in her hand, "You called the right guy Trevor." She dropped them onto her bag and took a shower. She dressed quickly still nervous that someone may walk in then slipped on her white sling back sandals and went down to find the car he'd given her to use. When she sat down in the driver seat she got a little thrill, she felt like a princess since he'd taken care of everything. Maybe it was time to thank Trevor for this; she dialed his number and set her phone down on the seat with the speaker phone on.

"Hey sis, how's the trip going?" he said with an excited lift in his voice.

"Really well, thanks to you. What made you think to call Max?"

"I think the guy deserves another chance, he has a safe place for you to stay and I think I trust him."

"I'm going to have to say an actual thank you. I'm really happy to spend some time with him. He's given me a car to drive while I'm here and I am staying in his room."

"Excuse me?"

"Don't get bent out of shape, we aren't together and he hasn't made a pass yet."

"Good, I'm going to get off of this phone before you make me regret my decision in calling him. Love you Veta." He hung up a little annoyed and she laughed as she parked her car in the lot of the conference center.

The next morning Max was in the shower and she was standing at the coffee machine he'd brought into the room for her trying her best to figure it out. He came out of the bathroom with a towel around his waist. "Good shower?"

"I'm clean so I suppose it went okay." He put on a comfy pair of pants and walked to her side with a familiar hand on her hip, "Did you enjoy your time alone?"

"Nope, this coffee maker will not work for me. I've tried everything short of flirting with it." She dropped the bag of coffee onto the counter. "Can you help me?" She gave him her pleading eyes.

"How can I say no to that?" He reached pressing a few buttons on the over complicated machine starting it. "There you go fresh coffee in only minutes."

"Damn rockstars and their expensive crap." She laughed walking over to a clear rug to do some yoga he passed her to sit on the sofa and watch.

"How much longer are you going to be in town?"

"Two more days then I'm out of your hair."

"So soon?"

"Yes sir, work is bound to be worried if I don't head home on Wednesday." She stretched down to touch her toes.

"Why do you have to live there anyway?" He lit a cigarette in hopes of getting a straight answer.

"I don't have to live there but I have a job so, I do," stretching her hands up to the ceiling and back to her feet.

"You had a job here, what went wrong at the hospital here that you had to move? Don't answer that," he left the couch to pour the coffee. "Is stuff happening for you in Denver?" he held out the mug letting her take it.

"I don't know yet. Maybe something is starting to happen." She looked at the floor knowing she wouldn't see any reaction on his face.

"That is really great for you, as long as you're happy. I won't worry about you then."

"Don't stop worrying about me all together. I'd hate to think I'd never cross your mind," she set her cup down feeling defeated.

"I am pretty sure you will never have to worry about that." He reached out to put her hand to his lips kissing it gently. "I just wish you happiness. Obviously you couldn't find it here."

"Can we not talk about this anymore?" she pulled her hand back. "Every time we see one another, this comes up and I just don't want to relive it all again."

"I'm sorry."

"I promise you, I won't fall for you again, but you have to stop drawing me in." she drug a hand through her loose hair.

"I invited you into the house, gave you a place to sleep and a car to drive. I wouldn't say I'm drawing you in." He chuckled trying to lighten her dark mood.

"Please don't joke around Max. You know exactly what I am talking about. You have a mysterious power over me and you wield it well."

"Turning phasers to stun for the next couple of days, scouts honor." He sat back on the couch trying to seem unbothered. "So, you met someone at your new hospital did you?"

"No, I didn't say I was seeing someone I said things were happening."

"It was an assumption sorry. Do you have any plans today?"

"I was going to jog around town for a while but I think I'll do that later when it cools down a bit." She balanced herself on one leg teetering for a moment.

"Would you prefer staying in?"

"Not really, it's just too hot to run like this."

"I can only imagine just how hard it would be to run like that, even in the fall."

"Clever." She changed legs, "I'd use both legs but I'd need a gallon of water.

"Would you like to go with me to a movie then?" His nerves caught in his throat as he waited anticipating rejection.

"That sounds like fun, why not?" it sounded like a date to her but he didn't make a big deal over it so maybe it wasn't.

"I'll see what's playing." He pulled a laptop out of a drawer and searched theaters.

"No chick flicks."

"That's right, she doesn't like girly movies. How do I forget all these things about you?" He asked himself aloud, scrolling through times and titles. "Well we've got three holiday movies, a cartoon and an action film."

"Action it is." She smiled at him.

"Now or later?"

"Shoot me some times." She stood over his shoulder to see for herself, her breast brushed his back and he stiffened imperceptibly to her. "Ah, let's go at eleven thirty." He bought them with a click and caught the smell of her hair as she pulled back.

"I should probably get dressed, you should do the same." He walked past her to the closet.

"Can you pick me out something to wear? The bags are really easy to figure out."

"Pick your own clothes. Reed isn't here and I have no idea what you even brought. Wear a pair of jeans. I love when you wear jeans." She obeyed him picking a strappy tank top to go with it and a jacket on the way out of the door. The movie was a thrill ride of adrenaline pumping fun that had them laughing on their way out.

"Would you like to go back home?"

The word home, felt so foreign to her coming out of his mouth and she just nodded. He was talking about studio recording and song writing as she asked questions. Nothing he said the entire ride made it into her thoughts about the way he'd said 'home' so easily. "Can't we just be friends for a while?"

He looked at her for a second trying to figure out where that came from, "Are we not being friends?"

"I meant do we have to become something more than this?"

"I have no idea what you are talking about but I think that you are under the impression that I want something here." He took her hand clutching it in his own. "We have had a long time apart, it's not like it was before and neither are we. I have to get to know you again and I don't really have enough time."

"I'm not going to be in Denver forever, it's just one stop and it's a good one. I have a few more months on my internship and I don't know if they are looking to hire anyone for the long run or continue to be a training hospital. Nothing is set in stone for me."

"Will you ever stop going to school and just settle down?" he said a bit impatiently.

"One day I may have to. For now I'm just doing the best I can to keep learning." His fingers tightened over hers. "Can you ever just quit the band?"

"Objection your honor, relevancy."

"It's the same thing, this is my passion and I have to pursue it to the best of my ability. I want to know everything."

19.

"Why do we always end up here?" She took a long drag off of his cigarette putting it back between his lips.

"The chemistry is undeniable." He chuckled to himself.

"Clearly," she said standing up from the bed taking the sheet off with her.

"No sense covering up now, it's all burned into my mind." He sat down on the bedside table tugging the fabric away from her.

"Someone is going to get hurt." He pulled her into his lap.

"That's later, this part is fun. We never spend enough time in this stage." He started kissing down her neck.

"Max!"

"Just play the game with me again, just one more time." He kissed her softly.

"No one ever wins this game. We're too old to start another round."

He moaned kissing her again. "Maybe this time it won't end at all."

"Yes and maybe the sun will set in the East for a change."

He took her face in his hands looking at her tenderly. "Stay with me Veta."

Her heart skipped a beat, "what?" She couldn't hear him as her ears filled with the sound of rushing water and radio static. His lips kept moving, in what she could only imagine was a perfectly sweet sentiment, but she couldn't hear anything. "What?"

His lips stopped moving for a second, "What's wrong?"

"I don't know I couldn't hear you."

"Will you stay with me?"

"Can I have a minute to process this? You, after all these years of telling me you're not ready, are ready? I move away and you decide you want me?"

"I always wanted you, we just never did the whole relationship any justice."

"We never had a relationship beyond hooking up every time we see one another."

"That's not fair we only slept together when we were dating and just now, and we talk all the time."

"True, but not once about this," She pulled on her dress. "You never made me believe any more than sex was going on here for you."

"I was trying not to put pressure on it and make us weird."

"This is pretty weird to spring on me. I've been straight with you all along about my feelings for you and it's always gotten shrugged off and forgotten."

"I heard it all, I didn't want to be tied down then." He stood to look her in the eye. "I always knew that when I was ready you were the girl."

"You were sure I'd be available, huh?"

"No, but if you weren't I was going to just forget the whole thing, stay single and live the life of a hermit."

"Max, I can't. In a few months when this internship is over, we can talk about this again. Please know that I am not saying no."

"I love you Veta. I can wait years but I have to know that I am waiting for you to come home not to change your mind."

"Can we try staying in touch the whole time and I'll promise more later?"

"That's fair," He dropped her hands. "I can't expect you to just trust me out of the blue like this."

"I wish I could."

"I deserved that." He pulled his shirt on over his head, "We'll figure all of that out later. I need to go to the studio this morning." He pulled her in for a hug "I plan on pursuing you, this time there won't be a break-up."

"Only time will tell, have fun at the studio. I have my own stuff to do anyway."

"Are you the speaker today?" he wasn't facing her but she knew he had almost forgotten just by the tone in his voice.

"First one of the day and I have about two hours to get there."

"Good luck." He turned to kiss her cheek, "I'm sure you'll be great." Then he left pulling the door shut behind him. She dropped to the bench at the foot of the bed to catch her breath. Had he really just asked her to stay? She almost passed out right there, thank goodness she hadn't. How do you act tough after face planting in front of someone? He was so serious about them this time. She knew this wasn't going to end well yet she couldn't even consider saying no to him. She took her time in the shower and put on her most professional outfit. Her make-up went on perfectly and her hair behaved well helping her to leave on time. The front seat of his black Cadillac was a comforting place for a short drive with its heated seats and steering wheel. She parked at the conference center and checked her lipstick one last time before striding up and swinging the door open. There were doctors everywhere, she looked and among them were some familiar smiles. Her Father's long time colleagues and men she saw all through her childhood at holiday parties. Those men looked at her now with lust behind their eyes. She was used to being stared at but this was a very creepy feeling. She found a seat and looked over her note cards making sure they were still in order. She'd never stood in front of a room full of educated people and spoke before at least not people she knew. These men had a tendency to be harsh as well. She heard her announcement and plastered on a perfect smile that scared the butterflies away.

The presentation went by in a haze as she answered questions accurately and pointedly, by the time she wrapped it up she was met with a round of applause. She wanted to sing, she was feeling respected and beautiful for the first time in a long time. She made her way out of the room and shoved the glass door open.

"You were phenomenal."

She looked up shocked to see Max leaning on the hood of the car, "Did you sit through that whole presentation?"

"Yes and I brought you flowers to celebrate. Good or bad, they're your favorite." He handed her the tissue wrapped tiger lilies.

"They are beautiful. I thought you were going to work today though."

"No, it was just one good run through of the final album, to make sure we are all happy and on the same page before it gets released to the general public."

"That rock star lingo is pretty hot." She sat down next to him on the very hot hood.

"I know. That doctor talk is damn hot too. Never tried to imagine what you do until today." He wraps an arm around her waist, "You're one tough girl, if I saw just a little blood I'd be uncomfortable."

"It's different when you know you could be saving that person's life. You don't see the gore, you see the mechanics of it all."

He brushed his lips over her ear, "That suit is so tight and sexy on you."

"Thanks, did you bring a car or are you confiscating mine?"

He chuckled, "I rode my bike," pointing over to a purple and silver Ducati parked a few rows over. "You can keep the car for now. How long will you stay here today?"

"A few more hours, I want to see Dr. Miller later and Dr. Sandiv will be up in the next half an hour or so." She was still smelling and pondering her flowers, "Will you please put them in some water for me?"

He took them from her, "I'll be out late, unless you want to go to a party with me."

"Hmmm, what time?"

"Around eleven, can you go out that late?"

"Of course I can I'm not a hundred."

"Well you could have fooled me, you go to sleep so early."

"I'm catching up from all the hundreds of hours I worked without sleep in the last couple of years." She folded her arms across her chest defiantly and pouted.

He kissed the tip of her nose, "We have to leave the house around ten, be really sexy." He looked her over again, "Or you could just wear that."

"I have an outfit in mind."

"Good, see you then. Have fun." She thanked him again with a hug and walked back into the building to find a seat. She tried her best to listen to what her mentor said while he was speaking but she just couldn't seem to focus. She was in her own head, a place no one should be alone with thoughts of Max. The man who was careful enough to skirt any kind of attachment to her for longer than she could remember was now trying to initiate a real relationship. She was left with all these questions. Was he serious? Would he wait for her to be ready? She couldn't stop wondering how she was going to get out of this. He wasn't ready for a real relationship much less a long distance one and he was setting them up for yet another disaster. On the other hand he had said that he loved her, something he'd never done before while they were together. Veta used to think that he was incapable of having feelings for her or that he was scared of that particular set of words. When instead it was because he didn't want her to love him? She still had trouble trying to figure him out. She had every intention of finding out what he was planning but until then she just had to wait and see what came to be. He wasn't going to change anything overnight.

Dr. Sandiv spotted her and winked, he was always such a funny man. The moment he was finished with his speech he hustled off stage to talk to her, "How are you holding up my dear?"

"I've been fine Doctor, I always enjoy hearing your thoughts on any subject."

"I'd forgotten already that I was up there. Are you alright?"

"I could ask the same?"

"Oh no I am, since my eyes met yours I've been thinking of your father's recent passing. Most people here are unaware. Are you alright?" He insisted again.

"Yes sir, I really am. Death is death and I know that I could have made no difference even if I was there." She shrugged, "I'm a surgeon not an EMT."

"I suppose you've heard enough about this."

"To be frank, I don't understand why everyone is making such a fuss."

"You look thin to me. Have you been eating?"

"All day."

"Alright I drop it. You were pretty good up there yourself this morning."

"Thanks, I was really nervous."

A large man came up behind her, "Ah, Sandiv you were a genius."

"High compliments from the director my dear man." He looked back to Veta, "I'll give you a call tomorrow before you leave town?" he squeezed her shoulder and walked away with the director.

Dr. Miller was sure to wow but she suddenly wasn't interested in sticking around all these stiffs. She was more interested in buying a good pair of shoes to go out in. She could only imagine who would be there or where it would be. Max had really gone the extra mile today, she was still skeptical about how serious he was though. The next thought was if she was ready to be serious with him, her career was starting to take off and she was enjoying being single for once in her life. She opened the car door spying a little note in the steering wheel.

V,

The moment you showed up in town I realized this may be my last chance to make us work and I can't let you slip through my fingers again. We'll have some fun tonight and I'll show you that I'm serious.

Adoringly,

Max

She smiled and started the car, on the radio was her favorite song and for the first few moments she just sang along and forgot about it. The next song was even more curious as she realized he'd put in a cd for her. Perhaps he had been listening all along. She was only in town one more night and she was determined to have fun.

As she walked through the mall in search of a perfect pair of shoes, she spotted one pair in the window of a nice boutique. The store was beautifully decorated and set up so that you could easily find just what you were looking for which ended up with her buying two pairs instead of one. His bike was in the crescent driveway along with three SUVs parked staggered around the bend. She opened the door slowly peeking in to make sure she wasn't interrupting anything. The boys sat at their instruments, strumming through the song she'd heard at the end of her Max made mix. They were a heavy band but with Martin's cool voice they sounded amazing. Max was the drummer and song writer but he could do it all.

"Welcome back," Matt waved with a smile.

"Just ignore me I won't interrupt."

"Nah, come sit down." Martin piped up.

She rounded the white leather chair and draped herself over it comfortably. "Do you always hang around here playing music?" She asked Mark who hadn't made a sound yet.

"We get paid pretty well so practice is kind of important."

"Isn't life funny, just a few years ago you were playing out of your garage for gum money?"

"I find it pretty interesting that a girl, who I once watched eat dirt, is now a doctor. The world works in mysterious ways after all." Max smiled but Veta was reddening by the moment.

"Tell this story please Bro."

"I don't think I'm allowed to tell that story but she tripped and had a mouthful of dirt once and it was hilarious."

"I guess I'm not going to the party anymore thanks though." She went up with her bags and put a darker shade of lipstick on then Veta slid in her tight red tube dress picking a black shawl to hang over her exposed shoulders. The tall black heels she slid on had just the right shine to catch the eye, her twirled hair sat the base of her neck wrapped in a red bow, grabbing her silver clutch to strut down the stairs. Max heard the clicking and stood up to see her walk, his jaw dropped. She was elegant, classy and absolutely gorgeous, leaving him feeling underdressed.

"My goodness you are a vision, can't wait to show you off tonight." He took her hand kissing it and spinning her around to take a better look.

"Thank you, where are we going anyway?"

"That party at the warehouse I told you about."

"Max, it's a dirt lot. I have to change." He held her by the waist.

"You will do no such thing. This is way too sexy to take off…unless I do it." He laughed and kissed her neck, "let's go,"

"Okay."

He called back into the house, "Martin, Matt we're leaving. Have fun." He led her out the door by the hand showing her the gold limo in the driveway.

"Did you honestly rent a limo?"

"Hell no, that's my car. I just paid my brother to drive us tonight. He wanted to go anyway."

"You are so sweet." She giggled stepping into the car and onto the slick black leather which didn't surprise her until she looked up at the clear window spanning the top of the car. "It's a reverse glass bottom boat."

"Congratulations, you are the very first person who got it." His door closed behind him as Veta lay out on the seat remembering once thinking of doing this for herself.

"It's beautiful."

He stretched out on the floor next to her, "Sure is, after a few minutes though the trees whipping past make you a bit dizzy."

"Oh," she sat up, "do we have a story tonight or are we invited?"

"We are invited, but we can create a back-story if you want."

She thought for a moment, "I think we're both interesting enough for this one, rock star."

"I'm going to have to agree, Doctor."

She looked out of the side windows as they drove over the bridge, spotting the lights and the hoard of people all around.

"It looks like they are just about to kick it up a notch."

She stretched trying to see, "What makes you say that?"

"Well, I'm about to arrive."

"But of course. Forgive me for overlooking your grandeur." She said without looking at him.

"Sometimes you are too close to things to see them. I'll be damned if I let you back up to do it though." He tugged her towards him resting his head on her shoulder to look out the window with her. "I sure hope you are ready to get wasted."

"No way, don't let me get stupid." The oversized car drove off of the asphalt onto dirt and parked alongside the building to shield it from view.

Mark opened the door with a silly grin, "Let's go kids, before the tequilas gone." He tossed the keys at Max and trotted off to the crowd flashing his laminated invitation.

"Someone is excited," he stepped out, taking her hand to help her out.

"I am too. It's been a really long time since I've been here." She walked unsteadily down the short dirt walkway to a 'velvet' rope lined with hundreds of people trying to get in. He walked right past them all with her hand in his. He gave the bouncer a fist bump, walking into the party.

She didn't know what to think of what she saw. The dance floor was a sea of people. Soon he was pulling her through the crowd to dance close with her. He wasn't any good but neither was she and they were having so much fun. After a few songs he leaned into her ear, "Let's get some drinks." She nodded as they danced off to the bar.

"This is crazy!" she shouted as he got two frozen daiquiris from the bartender handing them to her as he grabbed two shots, pointing out a table nearby.

"It's so loud over there." He rubbed his ears.

"Couldn't hear anything until now, you having fun?"

"Will be." He took the shot, holding his other drink, "This is going to make it even better…."

She stumbled in his front door shushing him and giggling, completely forgetting where they were. He pushed the door closed behind him reaching out to pin her against it seductively, "Let's go to my room and lock the door." Mark passed them both, giggling and going on up to his own wing of the house.

She whispered back, "How about we go and watch a movie?" with her fingers walking up his chest.

"Hmm, I'll make popcorn." He started to walk away but turned back, "Can you walk in those shoes still?"

"Pft no, I lost feeling hours ago." She teetered slurring her words, "I can hold my own though." Her ankle went out and she nearly fell before he caught her by the elbows, abandoning movie plans to get her into bed. He laid her down on one side, walking around to slide in next to her and watch her fall asleep. "Max, can you tell me a story?" she asked with her eyes closed and a sweet smile on her face.

"What kind of story?"

"A sad story," she said on a sigh.

"Alright, Once upon a time there was a queen who made all things in her path grow, her kingdom was lush with bright flowers and fruiting trees. The love of her life at her side all day, until one day her lover went to the fields to pick flowers and never returned. She knew not what had happened to him and in her grief and despair, froze everything in her path instead. Without his love to warm her she was left cold through and through, over the years her eyes glazed over and everyone looked the same to her, gray shadows of people that once existed so happily in their little world. How was she to know that he had been taken prisoner by her step sister in a neighboring kingdom unable to tell anyone where he lie? The queen of the castle he was trapped in would not allow him to see the light of day and the only thing keeping him alive was the hope of seeing his love again. One day after years of sadness and life in a frozen ice world of her own making she stepped out onto the balcony of her room to gaze into the sun hoping to melt down to nothing. The world below her jutted out with points of ice that seemed to reach for her. The shadows of her former land still walking aimlessly to find nothing to eat in the barren trees they once called forests. She was desperately broken inside and felt the out should look the same."

He glanced down to see her serene sleeping face. He had given her way to much alcohol but it was fun listening to her babble on and on about how she felt for him, made her look a little sweeter and more perfect to him. Those things would have never come out of a sober Veta, not even alone. She was so subtle and guarded at times and the life of the party at others. Damn him, for finally kissing her that night so long ago. He was never going to forget that night she was vulnerable and he had been there despite having a girlfriend. He kissed her goodnight before lying down with her to sleep. He'd thought so many things then, first and foremost being, 'what the hell was I thinking showing up here?' Easily answered the moment he saw her face in need tear stained and puffy eyed in the memory of the night. True he had no idea what to expect when she asked for company but she wasn't the type to cry wolf, she was tougher than that so he made sure to get to her when she did call for him. He shouldn't have kissed her but he should have mentioned Carmen earlier.

She wasn't a serious girlfriend for long after that night, he couldn't get V out of his head and Carmen was no substitute. He found himself conflicted, enough so to tell that girl that he wasn't willing to be her boyfriend no matter how many times she showed up back stage. Wasn't long after that he heard that another drummer married her, some people are only attracted to one attribute in a mate and clearly she was one of them. Max on the other hand was more interested in a single person than he was in anything she chose to do. Veta could have been one of a million different doctors and she chose to be a surgeon when she was seventeen years old and her mother had heart surgery. That day as she waited to hear whether or not her mother had made it through she decided that she was going to be the best surgeon in the world though at the time she'd said brain surgeon. Funny how he had thought so many times that it was silly for her to be at his house instead of at the hospital with the rest of her family.

Just then it dawned on him that the only person she wanted to see if the surgery had gone wrong was him. He had never tried to imagine just what made her stay so far away from everyone else when her parents later got divorced but she called Max every night and he shared with her father how she was doing. That was the only time Borris hadn't been rude to him or abrupt, the news was too precious and Max was the only messenger with it. Then when her father later died she hadn't called him at all, he heard from an anonymous source. Fate was the only reason they'd ended up in the same place that night and started talking again. Now he had to help fate along and make this relationship last the way he really wanted it to, the way he'd just realized it needed to be.

20.

Nothing made her happier than waking up in his arms, he held her so tightly to him all night, she felt the moments fleeting and wouldn't dare let go, if only to burn the feeling into her muscles to think back on often.

"Mmm, good morning Max." She twisted around in his arms to face him.

"Good morning is an understatement." He kissed the tip of her nose, "This is perfect." She wiggled free to stretch out and start some coffee.

"How happy are you really right now?" She tipped her head to line up their eyes.

"Pretty damned." He tucked an arm behind his head rolling to his back, "With a pang of sadness at the impending split."

"We both agreed that long distance wasn't going to be easy." She sat down on the bed again, "Do you think we can honestly do this without feeling torn apart?"

He drug her back down to him, "No, but how much longer are you contracted?"

"Two months," his unshaven cheek tickled her neck.

"Couldn't I stay with you for the last few weeks?"

"Don't you have plans?"

"The band is cooling our heels for a little while, just letting the album do its work."

"But you only want to stay a few weeks?"

"I was vague I suppose, I want to stay with you the rest of your banishment."

"Max, that's really sweet but are we ready to do that,"

"We don't have to if it's stressing you out." He leaned back to get a look at her face.

"I just need to be sure first, this has fallen apart pretty easily in the past." Max sat up.

"Veta, it was just a suggestion."

She took a slow, deep breath, "Getting a little ahead of myself."

"To be fair we are talking about the present."

"I know. If you think you can handle living with me, you are welcome to come."

"Not exactly what I was hoping for but I'm satisfied and now I can't wait."

"Do you ever not get what you want?"

"All the time." he lied, "Let's go watch a movie downstairs before you have to leave."

"That sounds like fun."

There, alone in his house they sat on the sofa watching a movie and cuddling or at least she was. She was focused on the storyline with the sporty cars racing around some foreign city she'd never heard of. He was in quite another race with his mind, he wanted to tell her so many things but what was he really trying to say. When this whole thing started again she said that she wanted to wait and see what happened after she was finished with her commitment, the end of that was two months away and according to her she had no plans on returning home or staying there. In turn Max was left to wonder what she was ready to be with him, when she said she loved him what did she mean? "Hey," she turned looking up at him, "Can we pause this?"

"Sure," she hopped up to get the remote she'd set on the table and hit the button, "What's on your mind?"

"I just thought we should talk for a minute," She sat back next to him on the warm couch, "We keep avoiding this big issue lately and I think that I'm ready to talk it out."

"I hadn't realized it affected you so much."

"Where you are makes little difference because I can get there... but who you're with is becoming more important by the day."

"I don't want to assume anything here, but aren't we supposed to be together?" She looked hurt and confused with the wrinkles in her forehead that got deeper by the year that he thought were perfect for her face.

"Yes we are together, I just meant in what sense?"

"Please just be straight with me here, what are you asking me?"

"Do you want to be married someday?" cleverly disguising the question.

"Depends on who asks me?"

"You are such a hard ass Veta." He sat himself up a bit more, "Do you want to marry me?"

"Gosh I don't know, you sure marrying a hard ass is the way you want to go?" He handed her a little blue box with white ribbon that stopped her witty running mouth instantly.

"Open it." She lifted the top off and tipped it to get the second spring loaded box to fall in her hand, inside was a white gold band with a beautiful pear cut, yellow diamond perched on top. There was no way to express the way she felt when she saw it.

"How did you know?"

"Trevor told me about the cut but the color was pure instinct, do you like it?" He asked hoping.

"It's perfect." She wanted to cry or jump up and down or something that would express the way she felt, "Are you sure you want to do this with me?"

"I can't think of anything else I need to accomplish with my life that I couldn't do with you by my side. For the last few years I saw that the only thing missing was someone to share it with besides my brothers. You are the only person who gets me better than I get myself and you still don't judge me." He scoffed, "What more could I want?"

"That's what I'm trying to figure out."

"Are you still proud of what I'm doing?"

"I am very proud of you."

"Do you still want to be a famous surgeon?"

"Yes."

"I have enough money to put you through any school you want to go to. You wouldn't have to work if you didn't want and I would be happy to travel to anywhere you might be learning when I can stop."

"Max, when will we be together?"

"When I have tour breaks and you have breaks from school."

"Wouldn't it be easier if I just moved home?"

"That depends on what you mean by home because from what I've heard you don't want to live at your dad's house."

"Couldn't I live in the house with you guys for a while?"

"You want to live in the big house? Please tell me you're serious because I'd hoped that you would since I really like that place and we've only been there for a couple of years."

"I think this is serious and we have to talk it all out now before I decide."

He couldn't get a seat on her flight and ended up on a plane two days later, which gave her plenty of time to clean the house up to her standards. When she landed, all she wanted to do was rush home and get out the best tablecloth and all the blue glasses that would look best against his dark wardrobe. Why would he want to hang out in some three bedroom cottage instead of that mansion with all the company, she laughed at the possibility of him avoiding them. Hailing a cab outside of baggage claim she hoisted her heavy bag into the trunk herself. He was a good driver, very quiet, if he said one word more than, "Where too?" she hadn't heard it. He did get out helping her remove her bag to the curb then tipped his ball cap at her generous tip.

The front step was littered with papers that she couldn't remember getting before she had left. She scooped them up and into the recycle bin before dragging up the luggage to get to work on the house. She pulled all of the gold candlesticks off the tables through the whole place along with their red dollies trading them out for blue candles and silver dollies. She lit up the house while she polished all of her wood furniture listening to dance music on the radio and sending messages back and forth with Max.

The work flew by with the silly banter they had about her cleaning addiction. He was never mean like everyone else was, though he did fall asleep before she was finished with her bed posts. He had been tired when she left since neither of them had slept the night before. Once she'd tucked away all of the cleaning supplies and showered to get the lemon scent off of her skin she slipped into bed to dream of him. Either way she still had to work the next day and try her best to stay awake.

>>>>>>>>>>>>>>>>>

She had to work a twelve hour shift to help out a fellow nurse and with the lack of sleep it was not what Veta considered an ideal situation.

When it was finally over and just thirty feet separated her from the Silver Beamer she never drove to work but Mindy was in the shop getting a new fuel pump or air filter or something of the sort and she didn't really know what else to do. Max would be on his own plane by now heading to spend a couple of months with her. The glass door slid open and on the other side stood Dr. Parks stomping out a cigarette like a nervous teenager. She felt like she barely knew him anymore but he recognized her.

"Veta, heading home already?" he stuffed his hands in his jacket pockets.

"I thought I would...what's going on with you tonight?" His actions were so suspicious she was clutching her duffel strap as if she might have to swing it at him and run but she tried to stay calm.

"I'm taking out a nurse from the burn ward tonight, she got off five minutes ago." He was still so confident even when he looked like he could have felt guilty for a moment.

She patted his arm encouragingly, "Have fun." There wasn't anything else she wanted to say to him or anything she felt she owed him but maybe she would let the nurse know that he was pretty controlling. She made it to her car and plugged in her phone that completely died in her locker that afternoon. She heard a few messages come in and set the phone to read them to her in its British narrator voice, each was a message from Max in various states of perversion. He'd been trying to be sexy but he always came off funny, it had to be the accent. She would have to read them again in bed after a long shower and some food. When she woke he would be there.

>>>>>>>>>>>>>>>>>>>>>>

"I proposed…" Matt stood there staring, "to V, gave her a ring and everything."

"What did she say?"

"She said yes, we've been keeping it to ourselves since she visited us."

"You turned a long weekend with your girlfriend into a proposal to a girl who doesn't even live at home?"

"Yes, wait what do you mean?"

"She moved away from home to be further away from you and her dad and now she is still there and he is dead. What do you make of that Sherlock? I'll tell you what. She's staying away from you now and only you."

"If that was true she wouldn't have said yes when I asked her to marry me."

"Asked who to marry you?" Martin was standing in front of the sofa with a steaming cup of tea in his hand.

"No one, forget about it."

"He proposed to Veta Iakar."

"VETA, you must be joking right? You've been back together for all of nine weeks and you propose?"

"See?" Max pointed to Martin, "This is why I didn't want to tell you guys, you should support me but instead you're trying to break it down."

"You're right, we'll back up so you can do it yourself." Martin snapped back and walked out of the room disappearing as fast as he'd appeared.

"Is this really how everyone is acting about me saying I'm engaged?" He brushed his hair out of his face, "guess I know why I've never done this before."

"You've had a chance?" Matt laughed.

21.

He had been trying to call her since he got to the airport that morning, even after he landed she wasn't answering and he hailed a cab to her house thankful that she had given him the key on her last visit as was the new rule, she had a key to the house in Chicago too. He was trying his best to figure out just what could have happened to make her unavailable to him, when the bright yellow Cadillac pulled up to her dark house he paid the driver, stepping out to get his bags he noticed that the garage door wasn't shut all the way. It struck him as strange but he forgot about it waving off the car and walking to the front door. Only the handle was locked and not the bolt, she kept the door fully locked even when she was home and things were beginning to feel less and less comfortable.

The sink had two mugs in it but nothing was out of place, her bed was made but her room was left open, he kept his hands at his sides until he made his way out the front door again. He didn't know what to do or what to think and dialed her brother's phone number trying to stay calm.

"Hello,"

"Hey this is Max, is Veta with you by any chance?"

"No, she took the weekend off of work even to get the house ready to see you." He stepped outside of the glass door of the store he'd just begun working in, "Is something wrong?"

"I just got here and her house is empty but it doesn't seem like she left because she wanted to."

"What do you mean? Does it look like someone was digging through her stuff or something?"

"There are dishes in the sink." He coughed realizing how feeble an argument he had for why he felt like something was so wrong but he hoped that her brother would have the same feeling about it.

"Call the cops," Trevor was nearly sprinting to his car, "when was the last time you heard from her?"

"More than a day ago and she has been calling me every day since I proposed to her." He wasn't sure if Trevor knew but it didn't matter right now.

"I'm on my way there. Call the cops and make a report and make sure they search the house top to bottom. Go next door and get Olga if she's home she's on the right."

"What's going on?"

"I'm not sure but she did tell me that John is there in Denver working in the same hospital she works in and the two of them had been friendly to one another." He was at his car trying to find the keys in his pockets full of promotional stickers and pens.

"What the fuck do you mean by friendly?" Now Max was starting to panic, if he knew where she lived and took her away then where was he.

"Cordial, I don't know call the cops right now hang up and dial the police."

"Okay." Max hung up and followed Trevor's orders, making sure they took the two mugs and checked out the garage door. He didn't know if her car was in it or not, he hadn't even walked into the garage. As the police instructed him to sit on the curb he decided to look for himself leaning as far back as he could to look under the door. The black car was gone and he still had the keys to the one that was left, something in his stomach said he had to find her, there was a tug on his heart that told him she wasn't okay wherever she was. What could Trevor still get his hands on and who could possibly help them find her? The answer came to him like a bolt of lightning but he didn't want to make the police believe he knew anything more than he knew before he called her younger brother. There were plenty of ways to find a person in the world and he wasn't afraid to dig in and use his money too. He was beginning to hope there would be a ransom or some kind of clue to lead him. The police wanted to question him but so far they just left him there at the curb sitting and thinking of just what he could do.

>>>>>>>>>>>

Veta tried to roll over in her sleep only to find that she was bound by the elbows and wrists behind her back and her ankles and knees were tied together too. She struggled a moment looking around in the dark room, there weren't any windows and the walls were no more than stacked cinder blocks mortared together in what she had to assume was a basement. Her head was swimming like she'd been drinking all night though she couldn't recall having a single one. Where was she, who had tied her up in their basement while she slept? She was terrified and helpless no matter how hard she tried to shake loose there was nothing she could do and so she cried silently into the cement floor praying to live through this somehow.

>>>>>>>>>>>

"Reed,"

"I thought I told you never to call me?"

"This isn't about you and I, someone took her they took her away and we have to find her."

Reed could hear the edge in the words and thought for a moment that it must have been some kind of joke, "Who took her Max? The mob, some home invaders tell me who you think did it?"

"John." Reed's stomach got tight and he wanted to be sick. There was no way this was a prank and he wasn't thinking about how much he hated Max anymore. Now all he could think of was what he could do to get her home safe.

"How did he know where she was?" Max told him all he knew and hung up after Reed said he was chartering a flight for him and Trevor for the next morning. There wasn't anything else he could think to do but he couldn't go back into the house and go to sleep, he opened the garage and pulled out the black car she'd had for ten years now to drive around looking for the new car she bought in the last couple of years. He drove through the neighborhood in the middle of the night just hoping to come upon it sitting on the side of the road or parked in someone else's driveway. In the morning he would go to see Olga and maybe she had seen something out of the ordinary or just what direction her car went down the street. There was no sign of a struggle inside the house and the things that were amiss didn't look so bad to the investigating officers but they didn't know her either. Those were his only clues and they were gone in some evidence locker never to be seen again or if they were it'd be too late.

Everything was too clean, something was so so wrong and there was nothing more he knew about it, he had his speculations but nothing that made any real sense. His head was spinning and he decided to pull over at a gas station outside of the community he'd spent the last three hours driving through. The cashier said the coffee was fresh but Max had his doubts as he took his first sip, he paid and showed the cashier a picture of Veta on his phone. "Have you seen her recently?"

"Not in the last couple of days but she comes in here on her way to work sometimes, usually with some scrub pants on. Is she a nurse?"

"She's a surgeon and a student a teacher and a tutor and a sister and so many other things but right now she's nowhere to be found. If you see her please call the police or me?" Max handed his business card over to the lanky boy who read it and looked back up with shock and awe.

"You're the drummer for Dis-integrated, Max Glenn."

"Thanks anyway kid, if you see that girl call the cops." Max didn't want to talk about his band or sign anything and walked out with his burnt coffee, back to the car. When he opened the door he didn't know where else to go and sat there calling her phone over and over to hear her voicemail message.

"Sorry I couldn't get to my phone, leave a message and I'll call you back as soon as I can." It was so simple. She didn't say her name or make it personal in any kind of way. There was a separation from who she was to him and who she was to everyone else, maybe it was just that wall he'd seen in her that was easily conquered for a man like himself with his smooth talking and honest approach. If he could just find out where Dr. Parks was living now he may be able to figure out where she was too. He never could figure out why they didn't press charges all those years ago or where that snake had slithered off to afterwards but it wasn't his business and he was trying his best to keep his distance at the time. There were a ton of things bouncing around in his head and only a few more hours before Trevor would show up with the only one of them with any surveillance experience the only one whose father was an ex mob boss who knew the world by their first names. He closed the door and drove back to her house with a sigh as he pulled into the driveway. He was exhausted but there was no way he could fall asleep in her place and stepped out the back door onto her patio, even the stars were lonely without her.

>>>>>>>>>>

She heard a door open upstairs and then footsteps coming towards them, once her eyes had adjusted to the darkness of the room. Her heart was pumping at least twice as fast as it was supposed to and her shoulders were searing with pain from the awkward position she was secured. She found herself wishing for a quick demise instead of the torture she was under in her current position. She heard a door knob turn and then a blinding light followed it into the room with the assailant hiding in the shadow he cast on her.

"Are you comfortable?" She could hear that he was smiling at her in agony.

"No, let me go please. I don't know what I did to you but I'm sorry."

"You have this very confused. I guess you don't remember me." He took a few more steps to her showing his face.

"John, I thought you were seeing a nurse at the hospital."

"No that was just a clever little story I worked up so you wouldn't suspect me to follow you home." He took hold of the rope dragging her to an upright position by the arms. "There aren't any alarms here, go ahead and take a look around."

"Untie me."

He cackled at the force she put into it with no way to back it up, "I don't see how you think you have any control here Doctor. You were always so confident but tell me Veta, whose coming to save you now?" He was right, there wasn't anyone who knew where she was, she wasn't even sure where she was and he hadn't told her anything to give it away. She was trapped with no way out and dwindling hope as his smile broadened on his face with the result of the terror he saw growing in her. "That's right there's no way out."

"I'll do whatever you want just please let me go."

"You'll do whatever I want? Is that the best you can come up with? I thought you were such an articulate person once and now I'm not so sure." He walked over a few feet to pull a bucket out to sit on next to her, in the waistband of the back of his pants was a pistol he was most likely going to use to kill her. Veta was trying to control her heart rate and think but all she could think about was how she would never see Max again. "I'll give you a minute to think of a better reason for me to untie you."

There was no way out of this basement in her position and he had that same look that she saw so many times before waking from the nightmare. "Why did you wait so long?"

"Starting a conversation, again not so original but I'll go with it." He scratched his head, "I think I needed to know more before I could show up at your house. Little Veta was always alone and honestly your security system isn't really secure."

"You watched me?" she was feeling less and less safe by the second as he thought about each step he had to take to get to this part.

"Not that closely I had to work you know?" he chucked her chin with a closed fist. "I took this," he reached into his pocket to pull out her ring, "seems there will soon be a Mr. Veta, did prince charming come back to sweep you off your feet?"

"I guess not," she sounded scared for the first time to his ears.

"So who gave you the Tiffany rock? I suppose it has to be either that red headed party planner of yours or the drummer." He sat there thinking to himself as she looked around for anything that she could reach but there was nothing in sight. "Must be the drummer, I don't think you would marry Reed even as a last resort."

"Should I make a dinging sound when you're right?"

"Are you going to fight now? I am so glad to see it, you were feisty too don't think I forgot."

"What are you going to do to me?"

"I've thought about a few different things but it'll be a game time decision." He laughed, "Why don't you go ahead and tell me what I should do?"

"You should untie me and fight me like a man." He slapped her hard across the cheek, bringing tears to her eyes.

"I don't think you're quite ready to understand the gravity of your situation. I'm in control here." She was shaking now and he was more pleased than ever. He turned around to pull a brown bottle from his jacket and soaked a white rag. She was tearing up when he turned back around.

"Please let me go John." His hand was over her mouth and nose with the rag she shook as hard as she could but she blacked out in a few moments.

>>>>>>>>>>>

The sun rose over the wall in the yard waking him in his uncomfortable position in the metal chair he'd dozed in. Reed and Trevor were due to arrive any time now and he went to the kitchen to make some coffee. He had never been in this house and didn't know where she kept anything, but the cabinets were well organized as he expected and it only took a moment to find what he needed. He made himself a slice of toast and ate it at the sink when he heard the door open and the guys coming in discussing something passionately. "I'm in the kitchen," he called to the two of them.

"Have you found out anything new?" Reed was in the room before Trevor with more panic then Max expected from such a serious person.

"Nothing, I thought you were digging on where he might have taken her?"

"I have a few addresses but they are all over the state and we'd have to split up to get to them all before something happens, or maybe it already has."

"NO," said Trevor in defiance, "Nothing has happened to my sister and we are going to find her and kill that son of a bitch Parks." Max didn't know what was on his mind but he tried to be supportive with an arm around his shoulder.

"I won't let him get away with this Trev, if it's him." They spent the next couple of hours looking over a map to find the addresses that Reed had pulled up on his search. They were both planning on renting cars but Max stuck with hers for luck as they were all leaving the next morning to reach the place each was charged with checking out. Trevor wasn't ready to think of anything other than getting her home and safe where Reed was thinking much worse things had already taken place. Max was of the mind that she was strong enough to fight her way out of anything as long as she could, Veta wouldn't give up. He prayed silently, please V don't give up.

>>>>>>>>>>>>>

Her arms were stretched above her head in opposite directions and her feet were pulled apart too as she found herself restrained to a metal table, another impossible escape. He was covering his bases as best as he could so she wouldn't get away this time. She was still searching her mind for just what to say to him if he gave her the chance to speak again. The tape across her mouth suggested he wouldn't though she knew he was a sucker for a good conversation, the longer she could distract him the better chance she had of figuring some way out of this.

What was he trying to accomplish anyway, he didn't want any relationship with her anymore since she had him arrested. There wasn't any reason why he should be angry with her since she dropped the charges and let him run off but something must have set him off. Was it the ring she so boldly wore to work that one day since Max had placed it on her finger? She was looking around now for the ring or any hints on what he was planning. On a standing silver table were a few instruments she recognized from her work in the operating room, a scalpel and a rib cracker next to some clamps and other sharp shiny things she'd never used before. On a white piece of gauze in the corner of this evil palate was her ring that appeared to have been sterilized, but why?

The door at the top of the stairs opened to John in full operating room attire, bringing down a lamp with him to light the room. "Good morning sunshine, I'm sure you're wondering what's going on." She tried to speak forgetting the tape across her lips. "Oh we'll get to that, I just want to make sure you won't pull yourself loose and ruin my work." He walked up to the top of the table tugging the ropes he used to bind her to the legs of the table beneath they seemed secure and he checked her feet too, tickling to make her struggle a bit.

"I should use less drugs with you, seems you've lost all that fight. Hmm, maybe being left down here for the day will sober you up more and we can have some real fun." He ran a clawed hand down her body trying to tear flesh and make her scream through the gag he wasn't satisfied with her reaction and turned the light off leaving her in the room alone again.

>>>>>>>

Max was nearing his location and the voice of the navigation system was directing him down dirt roads with no warning but when he got to the house there was no sign of her car but there was a rusted pickup truck in the driveway. He got out walking up and knocking on the door, the battered blue window shutters were half on the house that at one time must have been white though it was now a cracking shade of yellow. He peered in a window to see that the house was bare to the concrete floor and kicked the door before running back to his car to call Trevor.

"No one's here are you almost to your place?"

"This thing says I'm a mile and half away, head out to Reed's spot and help him."

"Alright, lines are open call me when you get there."

"Ten-four," Max hung up and got back into the car to reset the machine to the address he needed. He didn't know what else to do there wasn't anyone in the house and he had to find her, there was nothing else he could do besides hope that one of them found her and soon...

Trevor drove down a residential street in a little neighborhood in northern Denver to try and see if he could find John. He knew that if he found the guy he had a chance of finding Veta beyond any other chance alone. The little house on the corner didn't have any cars parked outside but he pulled to the curb instead, he opened the door and slammed it shut on his way to ring the bell. A little old woman answered and said she was renting the house from the young man who owned it and she wasn't sure where he would be, after several attempts to feed and hydrate him Trevor thanked her and walked back to the car pulling off before calling Reed.

"He isn't here or at the place Max checked out so you're our last hope, we're on the way." Reed hung up without a word and sped up with hope filling his heart for the first time since two days before. They were all racing on their own paths to the same place, Max and Reed were working together to do the only thing that they knew was right to do. How had they let this happen in the first place, it was Reed's job to check out all the people she was working with and make sure that no one had a history with her but John wasn't exactly an exotic name and it slipped by when he'd done the background checks. He felt responsible for what happened to her now that he realized he was and there was no way he was going to let Max have the satisfaction of knowing it was his fault. Trevor was mad enough at him already since he was privy to who had done the surveillance on her and it was obviously subpar and with a person as close to him as her it was worse than that still. Wrought with guilt in his sick stomach he was speeding around vehicles as fast as he could, luckily, without seeing any police...

Trevor was trying his best not to speed down the open highway he'd found that led all the way through this vast state, his sister needed him maybe for the first time in their lives yet he still felt he wasn't doing enough. There was some other clue he was supposed to be following, there was somewhere else he should have been going but he couldn't figure out where that would be. He'd found out that John's term at the hospital had ended two weeks ago and the place he was renting near there had a lease that lasted five months beyond that but it had a resident now. The fixer upper he'd bought in the last few months was empty only because he had something important to do somewhere else. He had a collection of old medical instruments that he showed off to anyone who visited his house. The first time that Trevor did he found it pretty disturbing to see a room full of sharp objects and cans of dental gas against the wall. He didn't seem that bad at the time since he was a doctor who could teach Veta some things and help her through school but once he attacked her all the possibilities went through Trevor's mind like a snuff film he hoped would never exist.

22.

It must have been hours that she struggled against the taught ropes trying to get even one hand free but nothing loosened them no matter how hard she tried. She wanted to scream but it made no difference now, she was sure he wouldn't have put her somewhere that she could have been heard by anyone and her mouth was still taped. What had Max done when he found her house empty? She could only imagine how scared he was with no idea what happened to her though if he could see her now he'd only be more worried. Would anyone find her body after he killed her in this house? Would anyone ever catch this sick bastard? She was whimpering in her delirious state with her eyes closed to try and think of something else. There had to be some way to talk her way out of this. She calmed down with a few deep breaths and started to listen to her surroundings. She could hear dripping water somewhere nearby and a couple of birds chirping on their merry way in what she assumed was sunshine, the last thing she heard brought on a new level of fear. A car coming down a gravel road from a long way off, she thought she must be in a very secluded place if she could hear it so clearly. She heard it slow down and stop in front of the house upstairs, he was back and she was doomed.

She waited trying to listen as best as she could but the footfalls were too quiet to be heard from her subterranean chamber until the door of the house was shut and locked. Something was tossed onto a table or the floor as she heard a male voice talking in an irritated tone though she couldn't make out the words being said. Her heart started pounding in her chest again so loud that she had trouble making out her own heart from his footsteps coming down the stairs. She closed her eyes trying to catch her breath through her nose, the end was near, she was a pessimist that way, there was nothing she could do now and she was preparing for the worst. A latex gloved hand took hold of her face roughly turning her head towards him.

"So you are awake." He laughed with the pleasure he felt in the fear in her eyes, "I've got to say this has been one of the best dates I've ever had, too bad I can't do it again." He started peeling up an edge of the silver tape across her mouth then tore it from her lips like a bandage. "So much better,"

"Wha, what are you going to do to me?" she stammered with tears already spilling down her cheeks.

"There are so many options, tell me Doctor how many organs can I pull out of you before you die?" He saw her try to recoil laughing again, "That won't work, the first thing I was planning on doing was taping your body to the table so moving won't be an option for you. Then I want to open up your rib cage and play with your heart like you did to mine."

"I wasn't playing with your heart."

"Save it, the only thing I want from you now is blood." He wrapped a thick heavy tape around her throat and under the table then around her stomach as tightly as he could to avoid messing up his incision. There would be no need for any drugs this time, she was going to feel it all...

>>>>>>>>>>>>>>

Reed was still a couple of miles from his destination and no amount of pushing on the accelerator was getting him there any faster. Max was only a few miles behind him and Trevor hadn't answered his phone in more than an hour. There was so much at stake here, what were they going to find if anything at all? He didn't know what to think and the drive was making thought less and less possible by the yard.

The house came into view and the mere sight of it had chills running up his spine. It was a huge Victorian house in bad disrepair with the porches barely hanging on. Her car wasn't there but he wasn't surprised since John wasn't an idiot. He parked a few houses down and dialed Max's number, "How far away are you?"

"Five miles, are you there?"

"I'm parked here, I don't think I should go up by myself something doesn't feel right."

"I'll be there soon, if he comes out stop him." Max hung up and hit the gas, Reed wasn't the type to have feelings about things around him since he was so often tuned into himself so the statement meant something to Max. Neither of them had questioned him since they arrived and everyone seemed to be getting along so far as long as they were working together. Still speeding down the road he was praying under his breath like he kept finding himself doing for the last couple of hours. This was the final lead they had and the last directions he had to follow before he stuck his head out the window screaming her name around the world until he found her. He pulled up behind the silver truck that Reed rented and got out to step into the passenger seat with him. "Any movement?"

"Nothing so far, we need to just go into the house instead of knocking. I don't think we should let him know we're here."

"How do you know he is here?"

Reed pointed to the back gate, "That's his van, he also has two trucks and a car."

"Do you know how to break into a house?"

"Come on," Reed pulled a credit card sized piece of metal out of his pocket and shut the door of the truck behind him. They walked together without a word and both headed to the back door since they so seldom had a bolt lock installed. Reed went up the two steps of the back porch and listened at the door for a second, there was a fan on but no movement that he could hear. He crouched down slipping the metal between the frame and the door which easily popped the lock open and sent the door on a slow swing to the wall behind it. They didn't see or hear anything, Max nodded for them to split up between the set of doors in front of them.

The wallpaper was new in the kitchen and the living room that Max walked through the carpet was an old orange shag he'd only seen in cars and there was a fireplace in the center of the room. He turned down an unfinished hall to a bathroom and then a bedroom. It was decorated for a bachelor or college student but there were dental tools lying in an open silver tray on the bed. He started to think negatively again when he heard Reed call out from somewhere in the other side of the house. He ran, with his heart in his throat and his stomach in knots to an open door leading to stairs, he took them two at a time grabbing a baseball bat from the stairway as he went. In the center of the room Reed had John pinned to the floor with a knee in his back and a scalpel to his throat. "Where is she?" as the words left his lips he turned his head to see her strung up and bleeding profusely. He snatched the instrument from Reed's hand to cut the ropes and tape holding her down.

"You're okay now, we're here." He tossed a lose piece of rope down to his partner who hogtied John then ran over to help him get her down. She was drifting in and out of consciousness and she was dripping with blood, so much that they couldn't tell where it was coming from. Reed left her in his arms to run up the stairs and find something to wrap her in and take her out of the house, he ran back down with a tablecloth. John was in tears hysterically repeating "again, again, again."

"Call the police and an ambulance, she's bleeding out Reed. I'm here V, I'm here stay awake stay with me." The tears streaming down his face made Reed kick John directly in the rib cage.

"You have no right to put your hands on me!" he screamed in pain, as Reed kicked him a bit harder.

"Why didn't I kill you?" He gazed down at helpless villain turned victim, "I'll do it."

"Call the police Reed, now, we don't have time for him." Max lifted her from the concrete wrapped in the white cloth, she kept her eyes on him though she couldn't speak or lift her arms. "It's okay V, I promise you are okay." He kissed her forehead cradling her fragile body up the stairs. He walked to the front door trying not to shake her.

On the front porch was Trevor with a whole swat team worth of people he'd never seen before, a pair of EMT's took Veta from him, he ran along to jump into the ambulance.

"Everyone into the house," Trevor commanded as the ambulance pulled off. Cops marched through the house taking John out the way they found him in the interest of saving time. Reed was the last out of the house and he was dragging his feet. "Come on Reed we need to get to the hospital."

"Burn it down." Trevor took his shoulder, "I mean it Trevor, burn this house down."

"Consider it done." He took him to the truck Reed had driven in and drove them both the hospital, she was still in surgery and Max was on his phone.

"I'm staying here indefinitely...replace me for the time I'm out...call that guy who worked with us in the studio when I had the flu..." Trevor sat flipping a nickel haphazardly into the air, Reed hadn't stopped pacing since they arrived, his mind was poisoned with a feeling of failure.

They let John live and she was still in an operating room, he had a nice cushy cell and she was hanging onto life. Why hadn't he just slit the sick bastard's throat, how much better would she be if he had just gone into the house instead of waiting for Max? The thoughts were consuming him as his paced the ten foot by ten foot waiting room.

Max hung up and collapsed into an armchair next to Trevor, "I can't stand this I need to hear something." He ran a nervous hand through his shoulder length hair.

"What do want to hear?" Trevor was obviously in another place.

"She stayed awake the whole way here, she even whispered hello once. Now I haven't seen her in ten hours and I feel helpless and stupid and I don't know what I'm supposed to do."

"There isn't much you can do."

"What kind of injuries did she have did you see anything?" Reed sat down on the other side of Trevor.

"They wouldn't tell me anything and they kept speaking their medical talk, the cc's and stuff like that." Reed should have been with her so they could all understand, Max didn't know any of those terms that the paramedics used so fluidly like a foreign language as he held her limp hand tightly in his. The three of them sat with pensive faces, possibly trying to figure out what they could have done differently so this never would have happened to her.

A doctor came out of a swinging door drying his hands, "Are you here with Ms. Iakar?"

"Yes sir," Trevor stood to shake his hand, "I'm her brother."

"She made it through surgery and she's on a long road to recovery, we had to close her up and give her a lot of blood and we removed this from her chest cavity," he produced her ring, dropping it into Trevor's hand, "In a half an hour or so she'll be awake and you can go in and see her."

"Thank you Dr. Foeman." He shook his hand again and turned back to the chair he was sitting in before. "She's alive, he says it may be a long recovery and they found this," He opened the hand and Max picked up the ring gently.

"You're engaged?" Reed asked in complete shock.

"I asked her a couple of days ago. I guess she hasn't gotten around to telling everyone yet."

"She probably didn't want me to know." Reed sulked still beating himself up.

"She didn't tell me either." Trevor replied with a hint of bitterness, "Maybe she was just waiting for the bottom to fall out." Max stood up.

"I don't know why she wouldn't tell either of you, seems you'd be supportive enough." He snapped back sarcastically.

"We are all hungry and snippy, let's go to the cafeteria and find something to eat then we can go up and see her." Trevor stood and took a step to Max patting his shoulder to get him moving. "Once we put her to bed we have a little mission of our own."

23.

Veta woke up in the stark white hospital room, there
wasn't anyone else in the room that she could see. She
was attached to an IV that was dripping at her bedside,
hung alongside an empty bag of antibiotics, where was
she now? She couldn't help but wonder if she was safe
though for a while she could remember seeing Max, or
had that really happened at all? A nurse stepped into
the room with a blood pressure cuff and a cheery smile.

"Just want to do a quick vitals check while you are
awake here, sugar." She put the cuff up her arm and
wrote down the results on the chart, "Can I get you
anything? Some water?"

"Yes please." She shuffled out of the room and
returned with a full pitcher and a cup with a straw to
set on her table near the bed. Veta thanked her and
asked if anyone was waiting for her.

Trevor's face was the first she saw, Reed came into the
room followed by Max and a huge bouquet he'd

bought downstairs in the gift shop. "Hey Sis, how are you feeling?"

"I'm alive," she exhaled, "that's better than I could ask for." Every word was slow and sounded pained.

"Aside from looking a little pale I'd say you're no worse for the wear." Trevor sat himself down slowly on the bed.

"If I look so good why are you being so weird?" She saw him try to think quickly and pushed his shoulder weakly, "I'm kidding, how did you guys find me?"

"Reed did his fancy research after Max found your house empty." Max was sitting down in a chair by the door, "Oh, hey come sit here I'll take that chair." Trevor stood up and took the flowers from him to set on her table.

Reed was in the chair closest to the other side with his head in his hands from the moment he saw her looking so frail. "You found his house, but how?"

Without looking up, "I found a couple of places he was renting, mine was the farthest and since we knew it would take the longest we left your house at different times and I was first to leave but last to find you."

"Reed," he looked up to her, "you found me, thank you."

"Don't mention it."

"Max, I don't know where my ring is, I'm sorry I lost it." He didn't say a word while he slipped it out of his pocket and showed it to her, "Oh."

"Do you want it now or should I hold onto it for you?"

"Keep it for me." She leaned herself up just enough to put her head on the side of his hip.

"We should go and let you rest."

"Can't you stay with me?" she said so quietly that only Max heard her.

"If that's what you want I'll stay."

"Well I guess we see where we rank here, I'll come see you tomorrow Sis." He came to the bedside and laid a kiss on his sister's forehead, "Feel better." He put an arm around Reed's and pulled him out of the chair, "Have a good night Max, you have our numbers if you need a ride."

"Yeah, thanks guys goodnight." They left closing the door behind them, "Can I lift you up for a second or will I hurt you?"

"Go ahead," he slid an arm under her and slipped himself down the bed to put her head on his chest and hold her close to him.

"How does this work for you?"

"I could stay here the rest of my life." She snuggled into him and for the first time she didn't want to go to sleep in the comfort, she wanted to stay awake and enjoy the feeling of his arm around her. "I'm so awake."

"Could you handle a question?"

"Yes, see I handled that nicely."

"Good job but what I really want to know is why you didn't tell them about us."

"I didn't want them to know because they both always have some clever comment." She yawned from the medication pumping through her IV, "If they tore it down how could I be sure it ever stood to start with?"

"I just told my brothers right before I headed out to you."

"How did that go?"

"I'd say pretty well but it would be a lie."

"So you understand then?"

"I guess I do. You should really try to sleep, I promise I won't leave you."

"Okay, goodnight Max I love you."

"I love you V, Goodnight." He laid there with her and closed his eyes. His mind threatened to wander but he stopped it quickly without much effort since he was thoroughly exhausted, he couldn't fall asleep though she was too fragile and he was afraid to move in his sleep and hurt her. There in her hospital bed he didn't feel like any kind of hero, they'd barely made it in time according to the lead surgeon. She'd been sliced up pretty well but carefully enough to avoid arteries and keep her heart beating. His exact words were "sadistically preserved her life." It made so little sense that this guy was somehow lying in wait to hurt a person as good as she was and he knew it was his fault the first time and now.

>>>>>>>>>>>>

"Where are we going Trevor?" Reed had been dozing in the passenger seat for well over an hour now and her house wasn't that far away from the hospital, he was finally awake enough to be suspicious.

"Those weren't cops who picked up John, the only thing real about that was the ambulance, not even the paramedics, though they are doctors so don't worry."

"I'm thinking you should slow down just a little and spell this one out for me." He scrubbed his eyes with the backs of his hands, "Where are we headed now?"

"A little place near the water."

"What are we doing exactly?"

"We're drowning the man who tortured my sister."

"Stop the truck Trev, that's no way to get even with him."

"Do you suggest we try to replicate what he did to her because that's not possible?"

"I'm not saying anything like that." Trevor pulled the truck over the side of the empty road, "She isn't going to get any better by us taking him out, but he should be in jail at least."

"So he should just serve his time and maybe in fifteen years after thirty or so appeals they put him to death in the prison. I don't think I want to wait for that."

"She is in the hospital with all those injuries and all that time we spent waiting and hoping that we'd see her again, I'm not interested in being involved in this and if I get out you will just do it yourself." He turned to Trevor with the most earnest look, "She doesn't know what you're doing but if she did she'd tell me to stop you."

"What, now you are trying to talk me out of it?" He pulled the key from the ignition and dropped it on the dashboard, "I took him from the scene of the crime and didn't report it to police it's already a crime either way so I may as well kill him."

"Trev, we can take him back there and call the police without much happening, they won't likely believe a psychopath's ramblings."

"Fine, I'll call them and have him brought back to the house tied on the floor like you left him." Reed nodded as he stepped out to make the call. He was relieved that he wouldn't be involved in a murder but more so that John might actually have to pay for his crimes.

>>>>>>>>>>>>

The next morning he was teetering on the edge of the uncomfortable bed as she slept painfully still on his arm. The nurses had been in at least ten times through the night and he was getting more and more tired though he still fought it off. At last her eyes fluttered open, "Good morning," he smiled down at her sleepy eyed face getting a smile back.

"Same to you," she moved from him in slow motion and he stood from the bed to stretch out his cramped legs.

"How'd you sleep?"

"Like a log, how about you?"

"Perfect, can I get you something to drink or a nurse or some pain killers?"

"Max I'm okay, I have some pain but it's just reminding me that I'm right here and I'm going to be just fine." He bent down to kiss her softly, "That's a beautiful way to remind me too."

"Only you could make this even the slightest bit okay, you're so optimistic."

"Can you put my ring back on please?"

"It would be my pleasure." He sat next to her and pulled the shiny ring from his pocket, her hand raised slightly from the sheets to let him take it in his own. The ring still fit her hand though it looked different in the shadow of the dark purple bruises around her wrists, "You are still willing to marry me after this?"

"Of course, the only thing I remember thinking the entire time I was down there was what would you do without me."

"There isn't much me without you and there was no chance I was giving up on looking for you no matter what happened I was going to find you." She just smiled at him and closed her eyes again still tired. "I need to go and take a shower and get you some clothes to wear when they let you go home in the next couple of days, will you be okay without me?" She nodded as she tried to fall back to sleep and he watched her body relax before he left the room. On the way down the hall he dialed his phone in hopes of getting in touch with one of his brothers.

"Hey Max, is Veta okay?" His youngest brother Matt answered.

"I'm leaving the hospital right now, she made it through surgery and she's resting, it could be a week before they let her go home."

"It's that bad huh?"

"I'll just leave it to your imagination and say I'm lucky she's alive. How about the surprise tour, you did the first gig last night right?"

"It was good, Jared lost the beat about three times but we recovered. I doubt anyone noticed that we had a different guy back there."

Max chuckled, "Well that sounds like things are going to be alright, I'll be here if you need to call."

"Yeah, we'll keep that in mind." Matt laughed and hung up the phone. Now the last thing Max needed was a cab ride to her house, the woman at the check in desk called a company and he thanked her walking outside to wait in the slow drizzle that had been going on since dawn. There was so much on his mind that he had almost forgotten that Trevor and Reed were at her house as well when he arrived around noon.

Reed was making himself a sandwich and moping around still feeling like everything was his fault, though he was having random moments of raging anger that had left at least one hole in the wall. Trevor was on his phone cooing to his new wife in a loving tone that was enough to make single men cringe but Max was glad to see him happy. He walked through without saying anything to either of them and went straight to her bedroom to take out an outfit or two for her, he didn't really know how to dress her and worried for a moment until he walked right into a packed bag sitting on the floor by the dresser. Reed had taken his own time to get it together for her with comfort in mind, with that out of the way Max stripped down and took a shower in her bathroom.

He'd have to find some way to sleep if he was going to be staying with her through the night but he couldn't think on so little sleep and ended up with a headache trying to figure the situation out. Max got out of the shower toweling off and getting dressed when he heard Trevor knock on the door, "Come on in."

"Hey Max, the two of us were heading back to the hospital if you want to come."

"I think I should take a nap or something I couldn't sleep there. You go ahead without me."

"Alright, the Porsche is back in the garage but we are still waiting to find the new car."

"Thanks," Trevor left and Max collapsed onto her over soft bed falling asleep within moments.

24.

When they arrived she had lunch on the plastic tray across her bed and a cheerful smile on her face, "Hey, how are you feeling now?" Trevor asked.

"About the same but I think I can almost stand up." She reached her arms out to hug him and then waited for Reed to come over as well. "What's wrong with you Reed?"

"I blame myself for this completely." He said with his arms still around her, "None of this would have happened if I knew about John being here."

"I didn't think anything of it because I thought that was in the past but I guess I was wrong, very wrong. Not you though you didn't cause this in any way."

"If you say so," he smirked a bit and sat himself in a chair near the bed, "When did Max put that back on you?" he pointed to the ring glittering on her hand.

"This morning before he left, I'm sorry I didn't tell you guys about this."

"Ah, what do we need to know for?" Trevor joked trying to lighten the heavy mood.

"In fairness you didn't exactly tell me before you put a ring on Ana's finger."

"That is a completely different situation and I don't really think you wanted to know before it happened."

"Ditto."

"Are you sure that the two of you can handle being married? You don't really have the cleanest of track records."

"I am ready, he says he is too and I can't ask any more than that from him. I love him Reed and I always have."

"I know you do it's just a surprise to me to see you so trusting."

"After what I've just been through it's obvious that I put my trust into the right people, sometimes the wrong people just get in the way." She pushed her lunch tray aside ready to just relax and spend some time with them. They talked about everything for the next few hours from growing up to college and how she wanted to decorate the wedding in gold tones instead of the traditional white. Reed started to show her pictures of dresses on his phone that he thought she should try on some day. Trevor was talking about moving back home to Chicago with his new wife and how they would live in his father's house like rich people even if they had nothing else. "I can give you the rest of your inheritance if that's what you need?"

"I thought you had already given it to me?"

"No I held back half of it knowing you were going to do at least one stupid thing and you'd need bailing out, I had no way of knowing it would be a wife but it's still in the bank for you whenever you need it."

"Did you save any money for Dalia and Shea?"

"Actually I did, they both got half just like you and I put my half on the mortgage of the house for the next couple of months."

"You really are a good sister, you know that right?"

"I try to be." She was starting to look tired again and the two of them left her to sleep.

"She seems to be recovering very fast."

"I couldn't hope for a better recovery."

"Don't you think it's just a little odd that she isn't asking either of us why we're here?"

"Reed, she isn't stupid and she probably figured out that we came to help"

"I guess you're right."

"She also wouldn't have blinked an eye if we both showed up unannounced."

"That's true too." He decided to forget the silly thought and just drive back to her house to wake Max for the night shift since no one wanted to leave her alone even there. The general decision was that Max would take over the daily care of her and when he was too busy one of them would fill the void but somehow they all knew that she would be alone again but hopefully nothing would happen to her. When that thought came up Max had suggested a security guard and it was shot down because she would never go for it. In any event she was going to be taken care of from then on.

>>>>>>>>>>>>>>

"Let's get out of here." She stood from the bed pulling the indecent robe from her body and stretching a shirt over her head from the bag Max brought with him, careful to hold it out from the stitches and staples holding her abdomen together.

"What do you mean? You want to go home?"

"I can't stand to be here like this, the only way I should be in a hospital is with a coat on not that damn thing." She hopped into a pair of jeans and swiped her bag from under the bed, "I'm healed enough and I want to go home."

"Can I at least talk to the nurse or a doctor or something and make sure that you aren't in danger of popping a stitch or something?"

"Sure that doesn't sound like a bad idea at all, you do that." She sat back on the bed patiently awaiting word of her release when a doctor stepped into the room with Max.

"I hear that you would like to go home, is that so?"

"I don't think I really need to stay here any longer I can take care of myself at home with all due respect."

"You've been in a pretty serious accident,"

"Oh it was no accident,"

"Be that as it may, we need at least a few more hours of observation to make sure you don't have any internal bleeding that we haven't addressed."

"I am willing to stay one more night if I have to but I can't promise any longer than that."

"Sounds like a deal, one more night and you can head out tomorrow morning if you see fit to."

"Thank you again Doctor I don't think I could have convinced her on my own." Max chuckled as he shook his hand.

"I'm sure you couldn't have." He patted his shoulder and left the room.

"So one more night and we can go wherever you want to go."

"Can we go home?"

"What do you mean by home?"

"Let's go back to Chicago together."

"That sounds good but I think Trevor and Ana live in your old house."

"Good thing that's not where I want to be, can't we stay at the big house."

"All alone?"

"What's wrong with that?" She winked lying back against the pillow beckoning him with a curling finger.

>>>>>>>>>>>

A couple of months had passed and she was spending less time working than she ever had before. The only thing she had to do was plan the wedding and it wasn't as hard as she thought it would be. Her dress fell into her lap from a boutique right in town that she and Reed had visited the day she got home from Colorado. The flowers were going to be light yellows and white, and the cake was going to be made by her sisters who had opened a bakery with the money they inherited. Max had lined up a few big bands to ask for the reception but she was set on asking his brothers to call Jared and play a few songs at least.

Trevor and Ana were going to be there along with all of her college friends and colleagues from Chicago, and even Olga was flying in for the occasion. Max hadn't left her even once since they had gotten back and he didn't seem to have any intention of doing so. She wasn't informed of the arrangement but if he was going to head out on another tour she was coming with them in the new bus she helped them pick out the third day she was home.

She didn't know what else to think about anymore except becoming his wife and testing the possibilities of happily ever after. His room had stayed just the way it was when she visited back in May, she thought about changing it but then she found a room right down the hall that was a much better fit for the time being. He still wanted to stay wherever she was and his room was used less and less. She had moved a coffee pot into the green room and even put a couple of pictures up on the wall. It was only the second place that she felt like she was really at home in all her life and he wasn't going to do anything to change it. Max was happy to see her so satisfied to be with him and he wasn't letting her go again for anything in the world. There weren't big enough things to promise him to keep him away now. When he'd taken her down from the blood covered tabletop he knew that if she lived she would never be farther than an arm's reach away from him not if he could help it.

The End

www.ingramcontent.com/pod-product-compliance
Lightning Source LLC
Chambersburg PA
CBHW051211120726
47905CB00004B/1071